She tried to ~~...~~
but her eye ~~...~~ ~~moved his~~
face right beside hers. She watched with a dry mouth
as he leaned forward to collect more flour from the
big bowl, the muscles in his biceps flexing with the
motion. When did they start building bakers like this,
she thought?

Pounding the dough with more flour, he wrapped
his hands around hers and continued to knead. "See?
You're getting the hang of it…that's it."

Sophie tried to focus on the dough and not the man
behind her. Beside her. Surrounding her.

"Push…pull, and turn." His soft breath was tickling
the hairs on the back of her neck. "There you go."
He spoke like a patient coach, and she wanted
to form something wonderful out of the dough
just to satisfy him.

"See, I knew you could do it." He turned and looked
at her, bringing their lips within inches of each other.
His minty breath was warm and she found herself
licking her dry lips, which brought his eyes straight to
her mouth.

They continued to stare at each other, neither breaking
eye contact for even a moment. Unable to stop herself,
she licked her dry lips again and it seemed to be some
kind of a signal to him, because he leaned forward and
gently touched his lips to hers.

Books by Elaine Overton

Kimani Romance

Fever
Daring Devotion
His Holiday Bride
Seducing the Matchmaker
Sugar Rush

Kimani Arabesque

Promises of the Heart
Déjà Vu
Love's Inferno

ELAINE OVERTON

Elaine Overton resides in the Detroit area with her son. She attended a local business college before entering the military and serving in the Gulf War.

She is an administrative assistant currently working for an automotive-industry supplier, and is an active member of Romance Writers of America. You can contact her via e-mail at her Web site, www.elaineoverton.com.

Sugar
RUSH

elaine overton

KIMANI™
ROMANCE

First, to my Lord and Savior, thank you for the many
everyday miracles you provide me with. So much of
what you do goes unrecognized. To God be the glory!

To my readers, I don't know how you all do it, but you
always seem to write me those wonderfully encouraging
e-mails just when I need to hear it most. Thank you all
for your continued support.

 KIMANI PRESS™

Recycling programs
for this product may
not exist in your area.

ISBN-13: 978-0-373-86111-8
ISBN-10:   0-373-86111-7

SUGAR RUSH

Dear Reader,

Thank you for taking the time to read El and Sophie's story. I've been wanting to do a mistaken identity story for a long time. I've always found something intriguing about the idea of falling in love with someone, learning all about them at a core level and yet finding out that you really know nothing about them on the surface.

I hope you have enjoyed getting to know the Mayfield Bakery family—Mama Mae, Wayne, Dante and Lonnie—as much as I enjoyed creating them. I love hearing from readers, so feel free to e-mail me at Elaine@elaineoverton.com, or write me at P.O. Box 51565, Livonia, Michigan 48151, and let me know what you thought of the book.

Until next time,

Elaine

Prologue

Sitting on the deck of his beachfront home, Alberto Montagna was having second thoughts about accepting his new assignment. Although in truth it was more than second thoughts, it was more like the seventieth time he'd told himself to call his agency and tell them to rescind his acceptance of the offer.

It seemed so unfair that he, Alberto Montagna, one of the greatest bakers of all times, was reduced to accepting an assignment in some small-town bakery whose only appeal was its lack of appeal.

You must hide, his lover, Carlotta, had said. My husband is a powerful man with a fierce temper, she'd said. He will destroy you in both name and body, she'd said.

Of course, the greatest problem was that she'd not said any of this soon enough! Actually, she'd said it after they'd made love and with the forenamed husband storming up the stairs toward the bedroom.

Alberto absently rubbed his puffy cheek. Good, he thought,

the swelling was finally going down. Lifting his lightweight tunic he checked the red, sore patches covering his flat midsection. They, too, were starting to heal.

He shivered, remembering the beating he'd received at the hands of Max Gonzales. Each punch had felt like a stone being pounded against his body. But the beating had not been enough.

Just as Carlotta had predicted, Max Gonzalez had dedicated himself to making sure Alberto could not find a job at any decent bakery or restaurant in the tristate area. Alberto had been seriously considering packing up his house and moving to Europe when his agent, Tom, had told him about a little bakery in Tennessee.

Tom suggested he take the job, lay low and allow Max Gonzalez to cool off. Perhaps if he waited six months or so, then he could return to his beloved Texas. It was a good idea. But, the closer it came to the time to commit, the more he began to reconsider his options.

Just then his cell phone rang and he answered. "Hello?"

"Alberto, my love. I have left Max."

Alberto sat up in his chair. It was difficult to hear over the noise in the background. "Carlotta?! Is that you, my angel?"

"Yes, I'm at the airport in Houston. My flight to New York leaves soon. Can you meet me there? At our special place?"

Despite pain in all parts of his body Alberto shot to his feet. "I'll be there by midnight, sweet darling."

"I'll be waiting," she said, her sultry voice sending an erotic thrill throughout his whole body. "And, Alberto, be careful."

Chapter 1

Memphis, TN

Carlton Fulton stormed down the long, plush-carpeted corridor leading to the office of the chief financial officer of Fulton Foods. It was midafternoon on an unusually hot May day and the roll of documents twisted in his tight, knuckled fist was moist with the sweat of his hand. His full lips were stretched taut against his somber brown face. Seeing the vein throbbing at his temple, his employees hurried in every direction away from him.

Without knocking he threw open the double doors to the executive suite that matched his in size and comfort. The startled secretary inside bounded to her feet.

"Good morning, Mr. Fulton." She forced a smile, but he could see the fear in her eyes.

"Is he in there?" he practically growled, nodding toward the closed oak-paneled door behind her desk.

"Um, yes, sir. Should I let him know—"

Before she could finish, Carl stormed by her desk and slammed open the door. He walked to the edge of the desk, behind which a young man sat, distracted by a phone call.

The young man on the phone was his nephew, Eliot Wright. Eliot bore such a striking resemblance to a younger version of Carl that many people assumed he was Carl's son and not that of his only sister.

The younger man glanced up with a puzzled expression. In answer to his unspoken question Carl held up the crumpled papers in his hand. Eliot slightly lifted an arched black eyebrow, his expressive brown eyes showing nothing more than mild curiosity.

Even in his fury, Carl found he was impressed by his nephew's unflappability. Eliot had changed a great deal over the years, Carl thought with pride. He was a strong, forceful man who got the job done no matter what it took, no longer the timid little boy who almost wet himself when asked his name. Carl took full credit for the transformation.

"Look, Steve," Eliot said into the receiver. "Something has come up. Just let me know when you get the meeting set up."

Carl tapped his foot rapidly, depleting what little patience he had as he waited for the call to end.

"All right, try to make it sometime this week. Talk to you later." Eliot returned the phone to the cradle and sat back in his high-back leather chair. "Morning, Uncle Carl. I would say *good* morning, but it's obviously not."

"It certainly is not!" Carl tossed the balled-up papers on the desk. "This is the third major account we've lost to that little hole in the wall. The *third,* Eliot! What are you doing about this?!"

Eliot picked up the papers and attempted to unmangle them as much as possible.

His eyes glanced over the pages and a low "Hmm" was his only answer as he read through the discharge letter from one of their major accounts. "When did you receive this?"

"This morning—by e-mail, no less! They didn't even have the decency to call and tell us they were canceling the contract." He leaned across the desk to point out something in the e-mail. "See that?"

Eliot's brows crinkled in confusion. "That can't be right."

"You better believe it is! Morningside, those smug bastards, wanted us to know just how much they were sticking it to us."

"No wonder Mayfield Bakery got the contract. That's an excellent bid." Eliot muttered, more to himself than anyone else.

Carl only glared at him in response.

Realizing his mistake, Eliot flipped through the few pages. "I mean, Morningside is a four-hundred-bed nursing home."

"I think you're missing the point," Carl hissed through his teeth, trying not to reach across the desk and strangle his nephew.

Eliot continued to read, seeming to have forgotten Carl's presence, but Carl knew despite his nonchalance his nephew didn't miss anything. And he had the uncanny ability to comprehend a complicated situation in a matter of minutes.

"This is the *third* large contract we've lost to this bakery. What are you doing about them?"

"I've got Steve looking into our options." He shook his head in confusion. "I just don't understand how they can afford to run their operation when they're offering up bids like this."

Carl's eyes narrowed on his nephew. "Hell if I know. That's what I pay you for."

He turned and headed back out of the office but paused at the door and looked back. "Eliot, I do not want to get another e-mail like that one."

Eliot tossed the papers down on the desk and sat back in his chair. "Don't worry, Uncle Carl, everything's under control."

"It better be. Do whatever you have to do, but I *will not* be undercut by some rinky-dink operation. Do we understand each other?"

Eliot nodded slowly, and Carl knew they were in complete agreement. For all his surface calm, Carl knew that his nephew was a win-at-all-costs individual. Eliot would be as ruthless as necessary to achieve his goals. He knew this, because that was how he'd raised him.

Eliot waited until his uncle left the office before picking up the crumpled letter and rereading the rejection of their bid and contract cancellation by one of their oldest and most reliable clients.

Although he'd hid it well, Eliot shared his uncle's concern. The amount of the bid they'd submitted to Morningside Nursing Home to service their kitchen and vending machines had been extremely low. They'd wanted to be sure to secure the contract, and yet once again they'd been underbid by the smaller bakery. It was the third time in three months they'd been outplayed by this particular bakery.

The first loss he'd chalked up as a fluke that could not be repeated. But after losing the contract for a private school, it had become clear they had a growing competitor they needed to take seriously. After learning everything he could, Eliot had put together a buyout offer for the competitor—a ploy that had been successful in dealing with previous upstarts.

That was almost two weeks ago. This morning when his uncle had barged into his office, Eliot had been on the phone with their attorney, Steve Ingerman. According to Steve, Mayfield Bakery had rejected the offer.

Eliot toyed with the crumpled papers, frowning thoughtfully. He'd hoped they would accept the offer, but of course he had a contingency plan.

Mayfield Bakery was a small proprietorship. Thanks to some recent upgrades in their equipment and the streamlining of their operation, they were now producing and packaging a unique line of cupcakes, cookies and assorted pastries on a much larger scale than previously possible.

The company was owned by a woman named Mae Anne Mayfield. She also ran the day-to-day operations of the bakery with the help of a small staff. And apparently the little bakery was doing so well they were now negotiating with one of the leading bakers in the industry—Alberto Montagna.

Mayfield Bakery was renowned for an exceptional line of pastries that both looked and tasted like they came out of some loving grandmother's kitchen and were made with the finest ingredients. But the operation had one major weakness—the small upgraded bakery could never produce the massive quantity of goods that Fulton Foods's industrial-sized bakery and packaging plant produced on a daily basis. The small staff Mayfield employed could never compete for the larger contracts, the hospitals, corporate businesses and larger school districts that Fulton Foods, which averaged a payroll of two hundred employees, serviced regularly. Not to mention the obvious drawback of such a "boutique" operation. The expensive ingredients, the manpower to process the homemade-like pastries had to cost a fortune, Eliot surmised.

Despite Mae Anne Mayfield's shrewd business sense and cunning, Eliot understood that no business had unlimited resources, and eventually the laws of economic nature would take their course.

But instead of simply waiting for them to go under, Eliot had asked Steve to set up a meeting with Mae Anne Mayfield. He planned to make an even more generous offer to buy the small operation and absorb their unique line of products and services into Fulton Foods. He would even offer positions within Fulton's corporate hierarchy to Mayfield and her staff for three distinct reasons.

The first and most obvious was that he could not afford to wait. The second reason was that what he'd seen of the Mayfield product was exceptional. If he could get the recipes and find more practical ingredients to produce pastries with the same taste and texture at a lower cost, the revenue potential would be unlimited.

Finally, Eliot would sell his soul to prevent future visits from his uncle, like the one he'd just received. Even after twenty years, seeing his uncle approach him with *the look* on his face could still send a shiver of terror up Eliot's spine.

He had to remind himself that he was not that same terrified ten-year-old boy. He was a man now, more than his uncle match in both size and strength. But the habits of a lifetime were hard to break.

For those reasons, he would make every attempt to absorb Mayfield Bakery, rather than destroy it. One way or another, through cooperation or brute force, Mayfield would yield to the greater strength of the largest baked-goods supplier in the Memphis area and learn what their predecessors already had: that Fulton Foods had an in-house enforcer willing to do pretty much anything to win.

Chapter 2

Meanwhile in Selmer, TN

"Sophie! Look ou—"

"Whoa! Whoa—ouuwwee!"

The loud crashing sound reverberated through the building and brought people running from every direction.

"What happened?" Lonnie, Sophie Mayfield's cousin, was the first to arrive. "Sophie, did you fall?"

Sophie bit her tongue to keep from lashing out at the younger woman as she stated the obvious. She knew Lonnie couldn't help her simplistic thinking. But with her leg throbbing painfully, Sophie was finding it hard to be sympathetic.

Wayne was immediately at her side, struggling to help her to her feet. "Sorry, I tried to warn you."

Trying to stand on her left leg proved impossible, as the sharp shooting pain raced up her spine. "Ouch-oww." She shook her head frantically. In too much pain for words, she tried to signal to Wayne that standing was not an option.

Apparently he understood, because he gently lowered her back to the floor. "That bad, huh?" His big brown eyes were filled with concern.

"What happened?" Mae pushed her way through the small group to find Sophie bracing herself against the walk-in refrigerator.

She gestured over her shoulder "I fell off that stupid step stool."

Mae pushed her flour-covered apron aside and knelt beside her granddaughter. "Let me see." As soon as she touched the injured leg Sophie howled in pain.

"Dante, call for an ambulance," Mae called to the last person who'd joined the group.

With a quick nod, the slender teen loped off to make the call.

"I'm sure it's just a sprain. Give me a minute. I'll be fine." Sophie smiled up at the huddle of worried faces. "Really."

To prove her point, she attempted to stand again, but the pain returned with three times the intensity, and a muttered curse slipped from her lips.

"Just sit your ass down," Wayne muttered in his gruff way. "You're not going anywhere anytime soon." He crossed the room to examine the step stool.

"I told you we should've got rid of that thing a long time ago," Mae said, shaking her head, her eyes focused on the rapidly swelling leg.

"You want some water or something?" Lonnie asked, wringing her hands in distress.

Sophie did not like the looks of that hand-ringing. "Lonnie, look at me." She used her stern voice to gain the girl's full attention. "I'm fine. Understand? I'm fine."

Lonnie nodded, but her eyes were still filling with tears.

Just then, much to Sophie's relief, Dante returned. "Paramedics are on the way."

"Dante, can you take Lonnie out front with you to wait on the paramedics?" Sophie jerked her head in the direction of the front door. Dante frowned down at her for a second, before understanding hit.

"Oh, right, right." He took the girl's hand. "Come on, Lon, let's go look for the ambulance."

"But, what if Sophie needs something?"

"I'm fine, Lonnie. Go with Dante." Sophie forced her most confident smile despite the pain coursing through her leg, and she breathed a sigh of relief as the two left the room together. The last thing she needed right now was a Lonnie meltdown.

Wayne grunted behind her. After five years of working together, Sophie recognized the sound. "What did you find?"

"The bottom bolt came out. Damn thing's rusted." Wayne gathered up the pieces. "I'll take it out back and dump it."

Mae watched him leave and shook her head once more. "Told you we should've got rid of that thing."

"I know, Grandma, I know." Sophie shifted, trying to find a more comfortable position, but nothing worked to lessen the pain.

"What were you doing up there, anyway?"

"Trying to reach those boxes." She pointed over her head. "Have Wayne get them down while I'm gone. We have to get that order for Centerfield Academy ready by Tuesday."

Seeing her grandmother's distant expression, Sophie frowned in worry. There was so much to do, and only Sophie knew that Mae Anne was no longer up to the task of running a busy bakery. A fact she'd tried hard to keep from the rest of the family.

She knew Wayne could easily manage the day-to-day stuff, but she needed to be there to help with the new clients. And then there was the new baker she'd hired.

The baker no one but she knew about. The baker they could not really afford but needed desperately. Sophie had thought it best not to say anything to the others until he arrived. Mae would not take well to being edged out of what she considered her kitchen. And she knew Wayne, Lonnie and Dante would probably be less than eager to accept an outsider, especially given his sophisticated background. Sophie knew she would probably have to referee for a while. Which was why she needed to be at the top of her game over the next few days, not hobbling around with a bum ankle.

What a lousy time for this to happen. "Grandma?"

Mae blinked rapidly, as if startled. "Yes, I heard you. Have Wayne get the boxes down."

Sophie nodded, satisfied that the task would be completed.

Mae's wrinkled face took on a troubled expression. "What if it's more than a sprained ankle?"

"It's not. I'll go to the emergency room, get a bandage and some painkillers, and be back here by nightfall." She reached out and touched the older woman's arm. "Don't worry."

Mae nodded in agreement, but it did nothing to allay the concern in her eyes. Just then Wayne walked back in from the alley.

"Wayne, I need you to get the Centerfield order ready to go." Sophie looked up at him, grateful to have such a competent assistant.

"No problem," Wayne answered, watching as the paramedics maneuvered the stretcher through the narrow hall that lead to the back kitchens.

"And keep an eye on Lonnie. You know she doesn't handle stress well." She sighed, trying to think of all the things that would need to be done in her absence. "And have Dante clean that tunnel oven in the back."

"Uh-huh," Wayne muttered, moving to the side to make way.

Despite his seeming lack of interest, Sophie knew from experience that Wayne's mind was like a trap and he would remember precisely everything she was saying.

"And if you have a chance can you review that contract for the Fielding wedding? Sheila Marks called this morning; apparently she and her fiancé are beefing again. Check the cutoff date for the deposit return." She shook her head. "This is the third time she's done this to me."

After checking her vitals, the paramedics gently lifted her to the stretcher. "Oh," Sophie added, "and remember to—"

"Sophie!" Wayne snapped.

Sophie's eyes widened. Wayne hardly ever raised his voice.

"I got this," he said, returning to his typical monotone. "I got this."

Sophie took a deep breath. "I know." And she did, but the habits of the last five years were not easily broken.

They heard a commotion at the front of the building.

"I'm going with you," Mae announced, pulling her stained apron over her head.

"Grandma, you don't have to. I'll be fine."

"Hush, child." She glanced at Lonnie and Dante as they led the way into the back area. "Lonnie, run upstairs and get my purse."

"Yes, ma'am." The girl hurried away.

Sophie started to argue, but what was the point? It was a well-known fact in Selmer that Sophie Mayfield had inherited her stubborn nature *directly* from her grandmother.

Wayne and Dante watched in silence as the paramedics rolled her down the hall leading to the storefront.

"Back to work, guys," Sophie called playfully. "We have a growing business to support."

"I want to keep you overnight."

"What?!" Sophie stared up at her doctor. "But you said you could just cast it and send me home."

"That was before I saw the X-rays." Dr. Michelson frowned at her over the top of his bifocals. "That break left a pretty nice tear, young lady. For it to heal properly you are going to have to stay off your feet."

"Fine—send me home and I'll stay off my feet."

He huffed in disbelief.

Sophie frowned. That was the problem with a small, tightly knit community. Sometimes your neighbors and friends knew you too well. "But, Dr. Michelson, I have a business to run."

"Well, it looks like Mae and Wayne are going to be on their own for a while." Dr. Michelson continued to scribble something on his pad. "I'm confining you to bed rest for the next six to eight weeks."

"Six to eight weeks?!"

"Sophie, I would appreciate it if you would stop screaming in my ear."

"Sorry. Dr. Michelson, but we just signed this really important contract. Is there anything you can put on it to protect it? I know—maybe if I were on crutches or even in a wheelchair…"

Eric Michelson watched her for several seconds before crossing the room to pick up one of the X-rays. Holding it up to the light, he pointed to a blurry white patch. "See that? That is the broken bone. Because of its location the healing could go either way. If I set it and you keep it still for the next six weeks, it should heal completely and you will be as good as new. If not, the bone will not heal properly—and for the rest of your life, you will probably have chronic pain in your ankle. Is that what you want?"

"Of course not."

"Then let me do my job. That bakery was standing long before you were born, and since I delivered you I can attest to that fact. Trust me, it will survive without you for six weeks."

Sophie bit her bottom lip to keep from expressing her own doubts about that. Before she was born her grandmother was a young woman working alongside her new husband, helping to build their family business. But today, her grandmother was an eighty-year-old woman with a failing memory. And Sophie had noticed that a few times Mae seemed to just stop paying attention right in the middle of a conversation. But when Sophie had asked, Mae was too proud to admit that anything was wrong.

"Sophie," Dr. Michelson said. He watched her with compassionate eyes. "You're a grown woman. When I release you tomorrow you, of course, can do what you want. But I want you to understand the price you'll pay for the stubborn streak you seemed to have been cursed with."

She nodded. What was she supposed to say? *Yes, Dr. Michelson, I want to be crippled forever.* As much as she hated it, she knew she would take his advice. It was the only reasonable thing to do.

As he turned to leave, her mind was already calculating what needed to be done over the next six weeks. "I'll go get you a room and let Mae know what's going on," he said. As he opened the door, Mae shuffled past him.

She wrapped Sophie in a tight hug, as if Sophie had been diagnosed with a terminal illness.

"The nurse in the hall said they were checking you in to the hospital."

"Grandma, I'm fine."

"I'm keeping her overnight to allow the cast to set, and afterwards, she's going to be on bed rest for six weeks." The doctor pushed his glasses up on his nose. "Mae, I need your assurance that Sophie will be off her feet for six weeks."

Mae's eyes narrowed on her eldest granddaughter, and she nodded with determination. "Don't you worry, Dr. Michelson, she will."

Sophie did not miss the small smirk on Dr. Michelson's face as he glanced at her once more before letting himself out of the room.

"Grandma, I left my cell phone at the store. Can I borrow yours? I need to call Wayne and let him know what's happening."

Mae dug around in the bottom of her worn purse and came up with the small cell phone.

"Where is your leg broke exactly?"

"Actually, it's the ankle. Thanks." She turned it on, and the phone immediately shut off.

"Ankle? Never heard of anybody breaking their ankle."

Sophie frowned at the phone and turned it on again. And once again it automatically turned off. Her lips twisted as understanding came. "When was the last time you charged your phone?"

"I don't know." Mae pulled a small stool closer to the bed. "Did you want me to bring you something to eat? Hospital food is so bland."

"Um…no. Where's your charger?"

"My what?"

Sophie frowned again. "Never mind."

She settled back against the stretcher, deciding to just wait until she was assigned a room and call Wayne from there. But, unfortunately, the useless cell phone in her hand gave her a bigger and more immediate concern than the goings-on at the bakery.

She knew her grandmother would insist on driving herself home, instead of waiting for someone from the store to come get her. She glanced at the window, where the light was already beginning to fade. "Maybe you should get going. It's getting late."

"No, I'll stay until they get you settled in for the night."

That's what I was afraid of. She twisted her lips, considering whom she could call or depend on to come if they said they would, and out of her large family there was not a single one. It would have to be someone from the store.

Sophie had bought the phone cell for Mae almost six months before, after having one of the greatest scares of her young life. She was working in the store late one night when Lonnie called and told her that Mae had not returned from a church revival she'd attended earlier.

Sophie called the police, and, being a small town, they were able to put out an all-points bulletin for the surrounding areas right away. Mae was found over an hour later in the next county over, almost a hundred miles away.

Once they got her home, a very shaken-up Mae explained that after coming out of the church, she must've taken a wrong turn in the dark, and before long she was completely lost.

That was the first time it really hit home to Sophie that what she'd assumed was a small problem could, in fact, be dangerous. So she had purchased the phone so her grandmother would always have a way to get in touch with her. But what use was having the phone if Mae never bothered to charge the thing?

A short while later, Sophie was settled into her room for the night and Mae was still sticking stubbornly by her side. Sophie glanced at the window nervously and noticed it was now completely dark.

And almost as if they shared the same mind, Mae announced that she was about to head home, just as Sophie knew she would. "Grandma, I really wish you'd wait for Wayne. He'll be here any minute."

"Why would I wait for Wayne? I drove my own car, remember?"

Just then, they both heard a slight knock as Wayne entered the room, proving once again why he was indispensable. Sophie frowned, as the harsh smell of marijuana preceded him. But she was so happy to see him that even his irritating recreational activity could not ruin it.

"Wayne! Am I glad to see you," Sophie said, grinning widely. Wayne paused as if surprised by the greeting.

"Damn, girl, what are they feeding you?" He reached up, gently touching the IV bag.

Sophie laughed. "Nothing you'd be interested in." She tried

to discreetly tilt her head in her grandmother's direction. "Grandma was just leaving."

Wayne's eyes narrowed briefly on her face, and then he quickly turned to Mae. "Um, Mama Mae, can you wait a couple of minutes? I was really kinda hoping you could give me a ride. I caught the ten-twelve here and that was the last bus of the night."

With a heavy sigh, Mae sank back down in the large chair beside the bed, with her worn purse across her lap. "Fine, Wayne, but I want to get home by eleven to see *Murder, She Wrote*. So, hurry up."

Sophie looked at Wayne and hoped he could see the gratitude in her eyes. Her grandmother would have someone in the car with her until she was within two blocks of her home.

With that weight off her shoulders she settled back into the hospital bed. "Okay, Wayne, here's the deal. That order for Centerfield has to be delivered by seven in the morning. Please make sure Dante understands that. He *cannot* be late. This is our first order with this school, and we have to be able to give them the same level of service they received from Fulton." *Now for the biggie,* Sophie thought. "I should be back at the store by noon, but just in case, we have a new—"

"No, you won't." Mae was shaking her head in a slow way that sent a bad feeling down Sophie's spine.

"What's that, Grandma?"

"I said no—you will *not* be back in the store by noon tomorrow, or noon the next day, or the next. You heard Doc— you are on bed rest for the next six weeks."

"Whoa, six weeks?!" Wayne gave a slow whistle. "What about all these new contracts you've stolen from Fulton?"

"I didn't *steal* anything; we won those bids fair and square. And I *will* be back tomorrow." She shifted in the bed to face her grandmother, and given the quiet resolve she saw reflected in the brown eyes she loved, she wondered if this was an argument best left for another day. "Grandma, I know Doc means well, but we both know it is impossible for me to take six weeks off right now." She reached out and took her grandmother's hand. "We have just taken on three of our biggest contracts ever. This is our chance to prove to the family once and for all that the bakery is not a waste of money."

Her grandmother's lips tightened and she quickly nodded in agreement. Sophie knew that this was the one argument she would not resist. Five years ago when Sophie's parents, along with her aunts and uncles, came together to try and force Mae to sell the bakery, only Sophie had stood with her.

At the time, the bakery was losing more than it was taking in, and no one wanted the responsibility of taking it over after Mae died. So, they'd gotten together and devised a plan to convince her to sell the store she'd opened over fifty years ago with her husband, Earl.

Unlike most of the family, Sophie understood that to Mae the bakery was more than just a means of revenue. It was the center of her life. She and Earl had managed to raise six children on the income from the bakery. When they first started off as a young couple unable to afford a home of their own, they'd converted the two small storage rooms in the back of the store into a living space. Sophie knew that the small building held more than just ovens and freezers to create pastries. It held the vast majority of Mae's lifetime of memories.

That was why Sophie had fought tooth and nail against her own parents to keep the bakery open. Against the combined stubbornness of Sophie and Mae, the family had not stood a chance and had finally given up.

And now, almost five years later, Sophie saw the chance to prove to all of them that she and her grandmother had been right to keep the store open. Now they had an opportunity to grow it into something more than a neighborhood donut shop, and she was not about to let a broken ankle get in the way.

Mae clutched her purse, obviously torn between her own desires to prove to her children that she was not a helpless old lady and the need to protect her granddaughter. "But, what about your ankle?"

Realizing she was winning the argument, Sophie sat up a little straighter. "I promise to sit with my ankle propped up, and let Wayne, Dante and Lonnie do the work. But, I *need* to be there." She snapped her fingers and turned back to Wayne. "When Dante comes back from his deliveries in the morning, can you have him clean out the apartment in the back? I'll move in there temporarily, and that way you won't even have to worry about moving me back and forth from the store."

Mae frowned. "I don't know if I like the idea of you being there alone at night."

"Grandma, I've already spent many nights there alone working on the inventory. It will be fine. The important thing is getting these orders filled on time, make a good impression on our new customers, and at all costs keep the bakery running smoothly. Wayne can you look in the office and double check the permits and make sure it's still coded for residential?"

"No problem."

Later she would blame the combined problems of a stubborn grandmother, and too many meds, but for whatever reason it wasn't until after Mae and Wayne had left that Sophie realized she'd forgotten all about the new baker flying in tomorrow.

Oh, well, she thought with a yawn, she'd be back in the store before his flight arrived. And he would need a ride from the airport, so that would give her time to prepare everyone. It would be fine. She yawned loudly again, as the painkillers took effect. It would all be fine.

Chapter 3

As Eliot entered the front door of Mayfield Bakery the next morning he collided with a thin teenager with a severe case of eczema.

"Excuse me" the boy called out, as he hurried away, his arms laden down with boxes.

Eliot turned and watched as the boy climbed into a beat-up, old van with a slightly confused expression on his face. Stepping outside, he glanced up at the sign that read *Mayfield Bakery*. He'd checked the local business directory on his laptop and this was the only Mayfield bakery in Selmer. This had to be the place.

He went back inside and glanced around. The glass counter was filled with fresh baked pastries, loaves of bread, cakes and pies. He closed his eyes and took in the delicious aroma. He hadn't realized how long it had been since he'd actually been inside a real bakery.

Fulton Foods, although considered a bakery, was in fact a large industrial machine that happened to produce baked goods, but it was not what Eliot considered a bakery. *This* was a bakery.

A breeze blew by him as the boy came back through the door.

"Someone will be right with you," he called over his shoulder, as he disappeared into the back.

Eliot stood in the middle of the vinyl floor, studying his surroundings and trying to make sense of what he was seeing. Could this possibly be the same Mayfield Bakery that had stolen three of his top contracts? Was this the Mayfield Bakery that was giving his uncle indigestion? Was *this* the newest threat to Fulton Foods? He almost laughed out loud as he shook his head in relief. Getting rid of this little shop was going to be a piece of cake—no pun intended.

The teenage boy came charging back through the store, his arms once again laden with boxes. This time he was followed by a short, chubby girl, also carrying a stack of boxes. She smiled at Eliot as they went by. She had a girlishly cute, light-brown face, but there was a blankness to her brown eyes that Eliot noticed right away.

The commotion and clatter of the back kitchen was easily heard from where he stood. He wondered if all that industrious noise was the result of their newfound business.

"Can I help you?" An older woman appeared in the entrance leading to the kitchen, wiping her hands on her apron. A slight smudge of flour smeared one cheek, and her gray hair was twisted and pinned on top of her head.

There was something instantly familiar about her untidy appearance. She looked like just what she was, someone's grandmother baking goodies. Or…someone's mother.

It suddenly hit Eliot why she seemed so familiar. He could remember many days coming home from school and being greeted by his mother looking just this way, right down to the flour-smudged cheeks.

He felt a rock drop to the pit of his stomach, because deep inside of him he knew without a doubt that this was Mae Anne Mayfield. Uncle Carl had sent him to destroy his mother's reincarnation. His lips twisted in frustration, like he didn't already have enough reasons to burn in hell.

"Are you Mae Anne Mayfield?" he asked, dreading the answer.

"I am." She'd started walking toward him when someone called to her from the back to the store.

"Mama Mae! I need your help now!"

Putting up a finger meant to hold him in place, she turned and scuttled back into the kitchen. Eliot waited a few seconds before following.

Slowly he entered the kitchen, not sure what to expect. He was shocked to find a small space crammed with new equipment. Everything from shiny, new reversible dough sheeters and dough rounders to bread slicers and stainless-steel preparation tables. The only things that looked worn and well used were two large convection ovens and the small, white kitchen stove against a far wall. On the opposite wall was a third, newer-looking double-decker oven, and a large, burly man was bent over and was peering inside the bottom oven.

"Damn this thing." Wiping his hands on a rag, he leaned back on his knees and looked up at the older woman. "I told Sophie I didn't trust that salesman. This thing is a piece of junk."

Behind him the teenage boy reappeared. "Wayne, I'm four boxes short!"

"I'm trying to—" The man at the oven turned to the boy and caught his first glimpse of Eliot standing in the middle of their kitchen. His dark eyes ran over Eliot's long length in one swoop, and then narrowed in suspicion. "Can I help you?"

The older woman turned to him, as well, surprised to see him in the kitchen. They were a study in contrast—the unsuspecting curiosity in her eyes and the wary distrust in his.

For reasons he would never understand, instead of simply announcing who he was and why he was there, he began to pull off his jacket. "I think I may be able to fix it—temporarily at least."

"Wayne," the teenager called to him again, "We are four—"

"I heard you the first time, Dante! But until I can get an oven going, you'll just have to wait. Now get the rest of the order loaded up."

"Why don't you fire up one of the other ovens while I try to get this one going," Eliot offered, as he kneeled beside him.

Without a response, Wayne jumped up and rushed across the room to start one of the newer ovens.

Just then a phone rang loudly, somewhere in the back. "I'll get it," Mae said, wiping her hands on her apron as she hurried off.

In his peripheral vision, Eliot saw the teenagers rushing back and forth, loading their arms with the full boxes and carrying them outside to the van. Obviously, they were on a tight schedule to get out an order and he had a pretty good idea which order it was. Tuesday was Centerfield's delivery day.

As he rolled up his sleeves, he considered how easy it would be to sabotage the oven and make the delivery incomplete and late. That alone might be enough to make the school cancel the new contract.

Reaching back in the oven, he found the coil he was looking for. Just as he'd suspected, it had dropped down and was causing the food to cook unevenly. He pushed it back up, a trick he'd learned in his first year working in Uncle Carl's factory.

Once he pushed the coil back into place he sat back on his heels. "There, that should hold long enough to finish your last batch. But you'll have to have a repairman come in and fix it permanently." He glanced over to find Wayne watching him carefully. Despite his offer to help, he could tell the man did not trust him. "With that oven, if you turn up the heat about two degrees per square inch for every fifteen minutes of cooking time left, it will finish in half the time."

Movement caught his eye, and he realized the chubby girl had come in and was standing in the doorway, watching him with her blank doe eyes.

Seeing the black grease smeared on his hands, Wayne offered his rag. Eliot took it gladly and wiped his hands, grateful for the knowledge his experience had given him. Despite the fact that he was Carl Fulton's nephew, he had worked his way up from the kitchen like every other executive in the company.

"Who are you?" Wayne asked.

"I think he may be our new *baker.*" Just then, Mae slowly walked in. Her head tilted at an angle as she gave Eliot a curious look.

So the new baker was supposed to start today, Eliot thought.

Wayne turned to her in surprise. "What new baker?!" Behind him the teenage girl was folding a box together, and the boy was holding a piping hot tray of bread loaves between oven mitts. Both froze in their tracks, and all wide eyes were turned to him.

"Apparently, Sophie hired a new baker," Mae continued. "That was the agency on the phone asking to have him call them when he arrived." Then Mae glanced at Eliot, her eyes showing the first sign of suspicion. "They say they haven't spoken to you since last week."

Eliot shrugged as if it didn't really matter, his mind working furiously, thinking how to use this situation to his advantage. The new baker would probably show up soon, but until then— whether he had a few minutes or a few hours—he could use the opportunity to learn as much as he could about the inner workings of Mayfield Bakery.

"Sophie didn't say anything to me about any new baker," Wayne insisted.

Eliot did not miss the slightly hurt tone of his voice. *Who is Sophie?* He wondered.

Mae looked up at Eliot in bemusement, then turned and hurried into the back office again. "I'm going to call Sophie and see what she has to say about all this."

Thinking fast, Eliot called out to her, "Could you give me the phone number to the agency, so I can give them a call? I don't have it with me."

She motioned over her shoulder for him to follow her.

As he passed through the doorway, he heard Wayne mutter to himself, "He doesn't look like any baker I know."

Eliot pretended not to hear the remark, although he was pretty sure Mae Anne Mayfield was the *only* baker Wayne knew.

As they entered the office, Eliot noticed a large, heavy-looking book in the middle of the desk. It looked like an ancient relic with its worn cover, which was pieced and taped together in places. He saw the word *recipes* scribbled across the top in black marker, and suddenly realized he was looking at Mae's recipe book.

There it was! Right there in plain sight for anyone to see…or grab. What professional chef in this day and age still used a recipe book? Most of the bakers he knew kept their recipes in custom-made software programs with two or more passwords protecting them.

For a baker or chef, their recipes were their lifeblood. For the very best, recipes were what separated them from the crowd. You did not leave your most precious treasure lying around in fat, album-styled books, Eliot thought.

Mae shoved a piece of a paper at him, and Eliot realized she'd been trying to give it to him for some moments. He accepted it with thanks, deliberately turning his back on the recipe book.

He started to leave the office, but she grabbed his sleeve to stop him. "I'm sure Sophie is going to want to talk to you."

Damn. Who the hell is this Sophie anyway?

Nowhere in his research had he come across that name. Eliot stood nervously by her side as Mae dialed the number. The mysterious Sophie could ruin everything with one word. Particularly if she was the person who had actually hired the real baker. His eyes strayed back to the recipe book. This was crazy. Why was he even playing this game? *Because you want her recipes—that's why.*

"So, the bakery business must pay pretty well outside Selmer, huh?" Wayne was leaning against the doorjamb with Eliot's suit jacket in his hand. "Here's your jacket. What's that? A three-four-hundred-dollar suit you're wearing?"

"I wanted to make a good impression," Eliot said with a slightly lifted brow. Intuitively, he knew this man was going to be a problem.

"Good morning, dear. How are you feeling?" Both men fell silent listening to Mae, whose first concern was for her granddaughter.

Eliot glanced at Wayne in silent question.

"She fell yesterday and broke her ankle," Wayne volunteered. "Otherwise, she would be here. Seems like Sophie is always here."

"Oh, that's great news." Mae looked around Eliot to Wayne. "She said they are releasing her around noon. Can you pick her up?"

"Of course," Wayne said without hesitation.

"Sophie, were you expecting a new baker to start today?" She glanced at Eliot. "Uh-huh…uh-huh… Well, why didn't you say anything to me?"

Now Wayne was standing straight up, his attention fully engaged. Glancing at him, Wayne's eyes met Eliot's for a moment, and it was clear to Eliot that Wayne was not a fan.

Eliot's mouth twisted in smug satisfaction. He hoped he could pull off this charade, if for no other reason than to irritate Wayne.

"Yes, he's right here." She handed Eliot the phone, and he took a deep breath.

"Hello?" he said, and waited for several seconds. "Hello?"

"Yes, hello, I'm sorry, I don't remember your name."

But Eliot did: Alberto Montagna. "You can call me El." He decided his nickname was close enough to Al, if it ever came up.

"Well, welcome, El. I'm sorry I wasn't there to greet you. Did you find your way to the store okay?"

Her soft, sultry voice was not what he expected. "Yes, thank you."

"Well, I know you probably have a lot of questions, and I plan to be back in the store this afternoon, so we can talk then. But again, welcome, and I look forward to meeting you in person."

The idea of meeting the woman that went with the voice brought a rare burst of excitement to his senses. "I look forward to meeting you, as well."

Handing the phone back to Mae, he excused himself from the office. Even after speaking to her, hearing her sexy, soft voice, he still wasn't sure who she was. She sounded young, but not too young.

He walked back through the store and out the front door just as the delivery van loaded down with Centerfield's completed order and the two teenagers screeched out of the parking lot.

He leaned against his car, dialed his attorney, Steve, and put him right to work discovering the identity of the mysterious Sophie. Then he called his assistant, Kara, to let her know he would be out of the office all day and to contact him only in case of an emergency. Then his last call was to the employment agency.

Eliot quickly introduced himself, and of course they recognized the name instantly. He then made a very large counteroffer for the talents of one Mr. Alberto Montagna, but only if the baker could start today. He made sure they understood that the offer had to be made immediately, even after they insisted they had no way to contact him. He gave them four hours to find the man. Eliot was assuming he would need no more time than that to get back into the office and grab the recipe book.

When he turned to go back into the building, he found Wayne standing at the glass window watching him. He considered what he must look like to Wayne in his expensive suit, standing next to his expensive sports car. There was a mistrust in the depth of those brown eyes that would not be easy to dismiss. His intuition was right as usual. Wayne was going to be a problem.

Chapter 4

Four hours later, and still no word from the agency. Eliot was beginning to suspect that Alberto Montagna had ditched his new job. Given the man's reputation as a self-important womanizer, Eliot had no trouble imagining what type of distraction could've come up.

As he poured the ingredients into the mixer, he kind of hoped the man *would* show up. It had been years since he'd mixed dough, and he'd forgotten what hard work it was. He wiped sweat from his forehead, feeling ridiculous for working in his suit clothes. The only saving grace was that it was summer and he'd chosen a linen suit and lightweight silk tie. After this day of manual labor both would be ruined, but what choice did he have? He couldn't exactly leave to change. He might come back and find his cover blown. Although, in truth he didn't really know why he was still there.

"Strange that a baker wouldn't bring a set of work clothes with him on his first day on a new job," Wayne commented behind him.

Eliot pretended to ignore the remark and started up the mixer. Mae was up front serving the walk-in customers, of which there were surprisingly many. The glass counters were constantly being refilled.

The teenagers had disappeared into the back somewhere after returning from their deliveries, and Eliot was starting to doubt the possible implementation of his original plan.

There was no way he could slip into the back office, not with Wayne watching him like a hawk. Then there was the problem of Mae. In just a couple of hours, she had him completely wrapped around her little finger.

Being in her presence had the strange but sweet sensation of being home again. Not his uncle's mansion in Memphis, where he'd spent the majority of his growing years, but the little brick house in Nashville. The only real home he'd ever known. The one he'd shared with his parents until they were killed in an auto accident when he was ten.

Mae felt like his mother and the women of her breed. Strong, yet gentle. Loving yet stern. All four of his grandparents had died before he was born, and he'd been cut off from his father's family from the time he was given over to Uncle Carl. He'd had a childhood filled with the luxuries of life but none of the warmth. Mae, or Mama Mae as everyone called her, was pure sunshine, and he enjoyed basking in it.

There was no getting around the fact that he'd come here for a reason, and that reason still existed, but Eliot was finding the idea of stealing that sweet old lady's recipe book becoming more distasteful by the minute.

A loud banging noise came through the wall. Unable to resist, Eliot asked Wayne, "What are they doing in there?"

"Cleaning it up. Sophie is going to be staying here for a few weeks until her ankle heals."

"You mean, here in the store?" Eliot suddenly had a bad feeling.

"No, the parking lot," Wayne answered sarcastically.

Eliot ignored that remark. He did note with interest, however, the news about Sophie staying in the store. That sounded like something an owner would do. That type of dedication was unheard of in a paid manager.

If Sophie was an owner, why had her name not come up in

any of his research, Eliot wondered. All his focus had been on Mae, and after what he'd seen today Eliot was almost certain he could custom-design a retirement package that would satisfy her. But what if selling the store is not her decision alone? What if she has a silent partner, one so determined to see the business grow she's willing to dedicate herself twenty-four hours a day?

All the pieces began to click into place. Sophie was the one who'd been seducing his customers away. Sophie was the reason for all this new equipment. Sophie was the one who'd rejected his generous buyout offer. *Sophie, Sophie, Sophie.*

That morning, as he was wiping down the mixer, Mae placed a perfect BLT on the countertop near him. "Thought you might be hungry." She smiled, and Eliot had an eerie vision of his mother's face superimposed over Mae's. The thin lines at the corners of her eyes crinkled as she smiled, the sign of a woman who laughed a lot.

"Thank you," he said, before pulling up a stool to the preparation table. "That was very thoughtful."

"It's no problem," she said. "I love to cook." They noticed Wayne carrying his sandwich out the back door.

"I'm going to pick up Sophie, Mama Mae. I'll be back in about an hour." He paused and glanced at Eliot, and Eliot could see how troubled the other man was about leaving her alone with him. It was hard not to like a man that concerned about a woman he wasn't even related to, Eliot thought.

He concentrated on his sandwich, trying to appear as harmless as possible. It must have worked, because Wayne finally turned and went out the door. Eliot smiled at Mae to let her know how tasty the sandwich was. And it was indeed.

But, the smile was also an expression of his satisfaction that soon he would finally meet the mysterious Sophie. The woman behind the sultry voice. The powerhouse behind the new and improved Mayfield Bakery. And hopefully Eliot would be able to fill in the last few missing pieces of the puzzle.

Sophie was more than ready to go when Wayne arrived to pick her up. Despite the painkillers, her ankle still throbbed. But even the pain could not distract her attention from the call she'd received earlier that morning.

Her new baker sounded like something straight out of a wet dream. He had such a smooth, deep baritone voice. Just remembering it sent a chill down her spine. There was no way he could be as fine as he sounded, she thought.

Still, she was eager to get back to the bakery to confirm or deny the fantasy she'd built up in her mind. And then there was that subtle challenge—at least, it *felt* like a challenge. Eight simple words: *I look forward to meeting you, as well.* It felt like he was saying so much more. But then again, the whole thing— the voice, the supposed challenge—could all be the sum-total effects of being without a man too long. Sophie chuckled at her own ridiculousness. All this over a two-minute conversation.

Just then Wayne came through the door. "Hey girl, you ready to go?"

"In a minute. I have to wait for the orderly with a wheelchair. Hospital policy. So, what do you think of our new baker?"

As if he'd been waiting for the opening, Wayne exploded in frustration. "How the hell you gonna hire a baker without telling me or at the least Mama Mae?" He began pacing in front of the bed, where she lay with her leg propped up on a pillow. "This guy shows up looking like he stepped out of the pages of *GQ*—"

"Really?!"

Wayne suddenly stopped and turned slowly in her direction.

Sophie cleared her throat quickly and tried to tamp down her enthusiasm. "Really?"

Wayne just watched her with narrowed eyes. "Yeah, really."

"But what do you think of him, Wayne?" she asked, leaning forward. "I trust your judgment."

"I don't like him."

"Why? Did he do something?"

Wayne shrugged. "Nope. Just don't like him." He started pacing again. "Although, I must admit he knows his way around a kitchen." He glanced at her shyly. "I've had him doing grunt work all day."

"Wayne! This man is a premier chef and I have the offer letter to prove it. Please don't tick him off." She looked him directly in the eye. "Whether you like him or not, if we are going to compete with Fulton we need him."

"I know." Wayne pouted. "After I got over being mad that you didn't even consult me, I thought about it. I know why you hired him. I just wish you had hired someone else."

"There was no one else, and if he hadn't been on hard times lately, we wouldn't have gotten him. So play nice."

He sank down in the big guest chair, frustration radiating from his pores. "He did fix the oven and help us get the Centerfield order out on time."

"See? He's already proven his worth. The old oven acting up again?"

"Yeah, we're gonna have to get that taken care of, now that we are doing all these big orders."

"I know," Sophie answered, wondering where the money was going to come from. "Did Dante get that back room cleaned up and livable?"

"Yeah, he and Lonnie have been in there all morning. Have you noticed how closely Lonnie's been sticking to Dante lately?"

She chuckled. "He's about the only one of us with the patience to answer all her questions."

"I don't know. I think it's more than that. I think you may need to say something to Dante, let him know that Lonnie's not like other girls. He might misunderstand her attachment, know what I mean?"

Sophie hid a small smile. It always surprised her how protective Wayne had become of them over the past few years. When he'd shown up looking for a job four years ago he'd been a recently released convict, and the hardness of prison life still clung to him. After he got over the initial surprise that he'd been hired despite his background, he'd worked like a demon. At the time, it had been only Sophie and Mae. Wayne had filled in all the blanks. He was the deliveryman, the fix-it guy, the heavy lifter and whatever else the job required, and he did it all without complaint.

It hadn't taken Sophie long to realize that there was an equally big brain to go along with that brawn, and she quickly put it to work, as well. Now, four years later, Wayne knew as much about

the business as she did, and she knew he could easily go somewhere else and make more money. But still he stayed with them,
loyal to a fault.

"Okay, I'll talk to him," she said, just as the orderly rolled the
wheelchair into the room. As she was loaded into the chair and
rolled along the corridor, her busy mind was racing. Sophie knew
much about their new baker's situation, and how he'd happened
to become available at a price she could pay. So her mind kept
telling her not to get excited. Of course he probably looked like
he stepped off the pages of a magazine, and of course his arro-
gance in his skill would rub Wayne the wrong way.

But even though she knew there was no rational reason to get
excited, her heart was still racing in anticipation, and she was
more anxious to reach the store than she cared to admit.

Eliot wiped the sweat from his brow and glanced at his
watch. Apparently lunch had come with a price, because as
soon as he'd taken the last bite, Mae had put him to work and
stayed to supervise.

A delivery truck had arrived filled with huge bags of flour and
sugar. He and Dante had been put to work unloading it. Lifting
and moving the heavy bags made his expensive silk shirt cling
to his torso.

He'd completely given up on the idea of stealing Mae's recipe
book. There was no way he could take a book that she'd spent a
lifetime building and protecting. Now his attention was completely focused on Sophie. Eliot had a feeling that stealing her
would be just as crippling as stealing the recipe book.

But what would happen when Wayne returned with her?
Sophie would know, wouldn't she? That he was not the man
she'd hired? And then he would be exposed anyway. So why not
just take the book and run?

As he watched Mae carry in a small box, he rushed to take it
from her. "Here, Mama Mae, I got it," he said, having already
picked up on the nickname the small staff called her by.

She smiled up at him with gratitude and brown eyes full of
trust. "Thank you, El, that was starting to get a little heavy." She

chuckled, reaching back to stroke her lower back. "These old bones can't do what they used to." She glanced down at his clinging shirt. "El, do you usually work in these kinda clothes?"

"No, ma'am, I don't." He laughed. "I just rushed off this morning without a change."

Eliot realized this was the problem. This woman, who reminded him too much of his mother. Her blind trust and acceptance of him was like a fragile glass vase that he was contemplating smashing on the floor. He had to do it. Uncle Carl would expect him to do it. But somehow he could not bring himself to do it, he thought.

He was restocking the box racks in the front of the store when Eliot saw Wayne's old pickup truck pull up. The moment of truth had arrived.

He climbed down from the racks and he waited inside the door, surprised by his own nervousness. It wasn't like Sophie Mayfield was truly his employer, after all.

As Eliot watched Wayne open the passenger door and help the young woman inside position herself on her crutches, he was surprised by her youth. She was petite, with long, brown hair pulled back in a loose ponytail. At first glance, she didn't seem to be much older than Dante and Lonnie. Listening to the others' descriptions, he'd expected something akin to a force of nature.

Using the crutches, she limped toward the front door, and Wayne walked at her side before holding the door open for her. Glancing up, Wayne's eyes met Eliot's for a moment, and it was clear to Eliot that Wayne was expecting him to be instantly rebuked. Eliot's mouth twisted, as he considered what the other man might have told her about him.

She limped to the entrance as the crutches bunched her shirt beneath her arms and Eliot found himself temporarily distracted by a smooth expanse of brown-skinned tummy revealed.

She stopped beside his car, looking at it for a long moment. Eliot would have paid anything to know what she was thinking. Then she continued limping toward the door.

In a way, she was almost as fragile as Mae, he thought, sighing heavily. These were no greedy moguls hungry for money and power. What had he wandered into here? he wondered.

As he was considering simply confessing the truth and reissuing his offer to buy them out, her eyes came up and met his, and all bets were off.

The sharp-witted soul that stared back at him from those eyes was no child. And Eliot knew in an instant that she was already considering the truth. That he was not who he said he was. He saw the questions in those amber brown depths, probing, and thinking. And Eliot knew this was his true adversary.

This was no sweet old lady who reminded him of his mother. His eyes roamed over her shapely form. No…nothing about her made him think of his mother. And despite her size and the crutches, she was about as helpless as a black widow.

She was gorgeous. Absolutely gorgeous. Everything from her large, almond-shaped eyes and sharp little nose to full, shapely lips that had him licking his as he considered how soft hers would be. All covered in flawless mahogany skin that had the pads of his fingertips tingling with the need to touch her.

She looked as if she should be traipsing across the state in beauty pageants, not here running a small bakery and becoming a thorn in his side. And Eliot fought a smile, as he saw desire reflected in her dark brown eyes. They fairly twinkled with surprise and interest. Despite his grungy appearance after a day of working harder than he had in ten years, she liked what she saw, he thought. Eliot wasn't a vain man, but he knew when a woman found him attractive.

Then she smiled, perfect white teeth so bright they could rival the sun. "Welcome to the Mayfield Bakery, Mr…"

"Montagna. Elberto Montagna, but my friends call me El."

"Nice to meet you, El. I'm Sophie Mayfield."

"Mayfield?" El frowned slightly.

"Sorry I wasn't here to meet you this morning, but as you can see something came up." She laughed. "The floor—when I hit it."

Eliot smiled, liking her already.

"You're back!" Lonnie came charging out of the back headed straight for Sophie, but Wayne quickly intercepted the girl and caught Lonnie up against him. The momentum knocked him back a step and Eliot realized the impact would've knocked Sophie down.

Two things occurred to him at once. The quickness with which Wayne stepped in to protect Sophie spoke of an intimate connection. Eliot didn't want to dwell on that. And the second was that Lonnie had not realized she would knock Sophie down. Suddenly the blank look to her eyes made sense. She was apparently mentally challenged. It was fairly obvious at first meeting, and the people who loved her were aware of her shortcomings and compensated for them.

From Wayne's arm, Lonnie's enthusiasm did not diminish even slightly. "You're back! You're back!"

Eliot watched as Sophie braced her body and nodded to Wayne to release her, and Lonnie threw herself against her cousin. Sophie shifted for a moment before regaining her bearing.

"Yes, I'm back. See, I told you it was nothing." Sophie smiled at the girl.

"Is the cast heavy?" Lonnie asked.

"A little, but I'm getting used to it."

"Welcome back, Sophie." Dante had come out of the kitchen behind Lonnie, and he was followed by Mae.

They all crowded around Sophie as if it were a family reunion and they had not seen each other in years. Eliot knew from earlier conversations she'd spent only one day away from them.

Mentally, he compared this small group of five to the hundreds of employees of Fulton Foods. The differences were like night and day, and yet this small group was now giving Fulton a run for its money.

It was amazing, really, and Eliot knew without a doubt the woman on the crutches was the reason why. She was the reason for all that new equipment in the back. She was the one who wanted to go after their contracts. She was the one with the ambition; she was the one who'd rejected their generous offer, not Mae. And therefore, as much as he might not want to, he knew she would have to be the one he brought down. And since he'd already decided he could not steal Mae's recipes, he had no idea exactly how to go about his mission. Especially considering Sophie, unlike her trusting grandmother, seemed to have suspicions about him. He only hoped his earlier phone calls worked.

"I was meeting our new baker." She gestured to Eliot.

"El here has been working his little heart out this morning." Mae came to his side, making herself his advocate. "Even though he was hired to bake, he has been a real sweetheart about helping me with the inventory all afternoon."

He nodded, his mind on the way Wayne stood protectively close to Sophie. It was becoming apparent that the two were close, and irrationally, Eliot found he didn't care for their relationship.

"That's good to hear, we like go-getters around here." Sophie smiled at him again, and Eliot felt his heart skip a beat. The woman really was too gorgeous.

"We got the back room all fixed up for you, Sophie," Lonnie said happily. "Wanna see?"

"Right now all I want to do is find somewhere to sit down." She smiled and winked at Eliot. "And of course, get to know our newest addition."

Sophie repositioned herself on her crutches and headed toward the back, the small group following patiently behind her, each giving her reports of what had happened in her absence. Soon Eliot was left alone.

Slowly, Eliot turned and followed the group as he replayed that smile and wink, and the possible implications of what she'd meant by *getting to know him*. He smiled to himself. This day was getting more interesting by the minute.

Chapter 5

Wow. As she settled into her desk chair, and placed her crutches against the wall, Sophie released a pent-up breath. *Wow.* Her new baker had completely lived up to the sexy voice she'd heard on the phone that morning.

She tried to focus on the conversation around her as Lonnie and Dante filled her in on every moment she'd missed. Her grandmother had said something about being hungry and left the room already. Wayne was standing in the door, half watching her and half watching someone in the kitchen; she could only assume he was spying on El. Wayne had made his feelings about the man perfectly clear, although she'd already decided to take his assessment with a grain of salt. After all, Wayne had a lot of alpha dog in him, and the thought of another grown man in what he considered his kitchen would have never sat well. Which was part of why she hadn't warned him ahead of time.

Despite his bias, he'd been dead on regarding appearance. Despite the dirt and dust, El did look like he'd stepped out of the pages of *GQ* magazine like Wayne said, and although she thoroughly enjoyed the whole package, the pieces didn't completely make sense.

For instance, she expected him to be arrogant and a bit of a prima donna. After all, he was one of the breed of chefs that considered themselves more artist than cook. Many of his type managed large staffs, as he probably did in his previous employment. So self-assuredness was expected, although this man *radiated* authority.

He looked as if he should be sitting at the head of a corporate board, not tossing dough in someone's kitchen. And he dressed like it, as well. What the hell was up with the business suit and slacks, she wondered. Maybe at Catalan's—the restaurant he'd last worked in—he'd been in a strictly supervisory position. That would explain his unpreparedness for labor. But, thankfully, he didn't seem to have a problem with hard work.

Then there was that sexy way he looked at her. Spending so much time in the bakery, Sophie rarely had time to date. But some things you never forgot. Like that flirty look he'd given her. And like the sex-starved woman she was, she'd reacted from the gut, instantly flirting back.

Then there was the smallest, yet oddest thing about him. His name. *El*berto? She was almost certain the résumé had read Alberto Montagana. But, a one-letter difference could simply be a typo, she thought. Either way, he didn't look like either an Elberto or an Alberto. Strangely enough, "El" fit him. And she found herself eager to be rid of Dante and Lonnie, so she could talk to him…and in private.

Lonnie was giggling and smiling at Dante, as he accused her of being the reason it took them so long to clean up the back room.

The bell at the front of the store rang, announcing a walk-in customer. "I'll get it," Wayne announced. He gave Sophie an I-told-you-so look and headed to the front of the store.

"No, it was your fault!" Lonnie laughed loudly, her attention still completely focused on Dante. "You kept playing around, throwing that box of packing peanuts at me."

"What packing peanuts?" Sophie asked.

"We found a big box almost filled to the top," Dante answered, stealing glances at Lonnie. "Looks like it was used to ship something here."

Sophie shrugged off the issue, discreetly watching the interaction between the pair. Wayne maybe on to something, she thought, because surprisingly Dante definitely looked infatuated with Lonnie, and Lonnie looked just as interested in Dante. Could it be the girl was sending signals she was not aware of? Maybe she would have to talk to Dante. She thought he understood that despite their being the same age and physical development, Lonnie's *mental* development was not where his was. Maybe she'd have to remind him.

She reached into her purse and pulled out a folded sheet of paper, handing it off to Dante. "My doctor called in a prescription for a wheelchair. Can you go pick it up for me? Here's the address."

"Sure," he said, pocketing the paper. "Wanna come?" he asked Lonnie.

"Okay." With a wave, she followed him out of the store. "See ya, Sophie."

Sophie frowned, watching the pair leave. They were too close. How had she not seen the relationship growing? But she hadn't. Not until Wayne mentioned it. But, truth be told, she didn't pay much attention to Lonnie—not nearly as much as she should, she thought guiltily.

Lonnie had been a victim of circumstance almost from the moment she'd been conceived. She was the daughter of Mae's firstborn, Sharyn, who'd been into one thing or another since her teen years, according to family gossip.

Sophie didn't know her mother's older sister very well, because she'd been banned from their home most of Sophie's life. But when Sharyn came up pregnant at the age of forty-one, everyone in the family was concerned, given her track record. And eventually, the concern was proven valid when Lonnie had been diagnosed with Down syndrome.

When Lonnie was born, Sharyn apparently did try to be a good mother for a while, but soon the responsibility of caring for a mentally challenged child became too much for her. Somehow—no one really remembered—Lonnie ended up in the collective hands of the family, eventually landing at the door of her grandmother, with whom she'd lived the past six years.

As far back as Sophie could remember, Lonnie had tagged after her like a little sister, desperate for attention and approval. And, although no one ever said it, Sophie did feel a certain responsibility for the girl.

Mae reappeared in the door with a plate laden with so much food Sophie's eyes widened in concern. "Grandma! What am I suppose to do with all that food?"

Mae gave a look that seemed to question Sophie's sanity. "What anybody would do. Eat it."

Sophie shook her head. "I will never understand why you and Granddad opened a bakery instead of a restaurant. The way you like to cook…"

Mae's age-worn face took on a softer look as she remembered her long-dead husband. "That bakery was your granddaddy's idea—and it wasn't his first, let me tell you! We tried a laundry service at one time, and we even tried a grocer's store. None of it ever amounted to much." She chuckled to herself. Sophie listened patiently with a smile, thinking of the man she had only the vaguest memories of. She'd heard all the stories of her grandparents' failed business ventures a dozen times. Sophie also knew it was part of what kept her parents, aunts and uncles from stepping in to help when the bakery started going under.

"Your granddaddy never had much of a head for business, but he had ideas and more ideas!" She looked at Sophie with a playful grin. "And I loved him so much, he could've wanted to sell sand in a desert and I would've been right there beside him."

She reached out and touched her granddaughter's face. "You remind me so much of him, always with ideas." She bent and placed a quick kiss on her forehead. "Now you just have to find a man you can sell sand to." With a chuckle, she turned and walked out, wiping her hands on her apron, the habit of a lifetime.

And for the first time since she'd limped into the front door, Sophie found herself completely alone with her thoughts. Once again they wandered back to her handsome new baker.

With his copper golden skin and eyes that matched, he could've been the love child of Apollo, the sun god. He wore his hair in short locks, which were an unusual sandy brown. With his skin tone the color was likely natural. El did not look like the hair-dye kind of brother.

He was tall, maybe six feet plus, and tended toward lean except in the shoulders, which were bunched with muscles visible even beneath the thin material of his shirt. Another factor that would rankle Wayne. The ex-convict was built like a bulldog, short and stocky.

At first glance, she'd thought El was younger, closer to her age. But one look in his eyes, and there she found a man who knew something of life. Top all that lusciousness off with beautiful, perfect, bubble-gum-pink lips and he was scrumptious enough to go in the counter next to any of the confectionary treats there.

She heard a light rap on the door and jumped, slightly startled to see El standing there smiling at her, as if summoned by her thoughts.

He glanced at the plate of food. "I see Mama Mae's struck already."

Sophie laughed. "Yeah. You'd think after a lifetime of her cooking, I'd be as big as a house."

His eyes roamed over her body appreciatively, as he said, "No but it looks like you filled out in all the right places."

Sophie decided to ignore the remark. They were already getting off to a less-than-professional start. She reached over and pulled up a chair. "Got a minute? I was hoping we could talk."

"Sure." He took a seat, leaning forward slightly. "You sure you should be here? Just getting out of the hospital and all?"

"'Should' is not the issue. I need to be here. We have just taken on a lot of big contracts including Morningside. We even outbid our competition—"

"Your competition?"

"Fulton Foods, out of Memphis. Heard of them?"

"Yeah, I think I have. But they're a really big operation." He frowned. "No offense, but are you really capable of competing with them?"

She bit her bottom lip. "Honestly—no. But we are going to give it a hell of a try. How else can we grow? The market we're in is saturated. There are dozens of small neighborhood bakeries in this area. But Fulton has a monopoly on all the larger contracts." She counted off on her fingers. "The schools, hospitals, municipalities. If we can just get these first few contracts fulfilled to each client's satisfaction, we can start building some reputation equity. Does that make any sense?"

His eyes had narrowed on her face as he listened intently. "Yes, sorta like a fighter training to move into a different weight category. Light to middle, middle to heavy."

She laughed. "Exactly! That's a terrific analogy. And that's where you come in." She looked directly at him. "If we are going to be a premier bakery, we need a premier chef."

He nodded, looking down at the floor. "I'm flattered, but I must admit that I don't see the need. Mama Mae's pastries are exceptional. The quality and taste could compete with anything Fulton puts out."

Sophie glanced at the door. "My grandmother is a talented baker, but she's not a young woman, El. She's getting up in age, and sometimes she…sometimes she forgets things. We are really going to be under the gun in the next few months, and I don't want that kind of pressure on her." She reached over and laid her hand on the big recipe book. "I was hoping you could take a look at her book and learn the basics as well as some of the fancier designs she doesn't really do on a daily basis. And we'll incorporate those into our new menu."

El's eyes came up to hers in surprise. "You want me to learn her recipes?" He glanced at the door. "Is she okay with that?"

Sophie smiled. "Look, I know where you come from must be ultracompetitive, and bakers would probably kill before revealing their recipes. But my grandmother bakes and cooks because she loves it. Truth is, she'd probably give the stuff away if she could." She shook her head. "There is not a competitive bone in her body. I only ask that you not share her recipes. My grandmother may not care one way or the other, but those recipes are the lifeblood of this bakery. Without them we would be destroyed."

El nodded slowly, thoughtfully.

He understood, she thought. "Good. Now is there anything you would like from me?"

El stood. "No, that pretty much covers it."

"Oh, wait!" She reached across the desk and picked up a manila folder. "I need you to fill out the contact sheet and tax forms. And your health insurance information is inside, as well."

"You offer medical benefits?" he asked, opening the folder.

"Yes. Didn't Tom tell you that?"

"Yes—of course. It must've slipped my mind." He glanced through the pages. "It probably cost you a fortune with such a small staff."

She shrugged. "It ain't cheap, but I owe it to them. I owe it to you."

Eliot just looked at her for several moments, and she had no idea what he was thinking. It wasn't like the flirty little look he'd given her earlier. This look was more like he was trying to work something out in his head. Although she had no idea what. "Everything okay?"

He nodded and held up the folder. "I'll read it over and bring it back tomorrow."

"Oh wait." Sophie reached over and tried to pick up the recipe book, but it was too heavy. "Did you want to take the recipe book with you to look over tonight?"

He stared at the book for several long seconds, just the way he'd stared at her, and finally shook his head. "No, I'll look it over later." He started to leave again, and paused. "Um, I may not be in tomorrow."

She started to protest but held back. The man had just arrived in town. Of course he would need some time to get himself settled. As much as they needed his skills, it was only fair to give him some time.

"Sure, no problem," she said. "And El, again, welcome. I know this is not the type of environment you are used to working in, but I think if you give us a chance we could win you over." She gave him a cheeky grin.

He answered with a soft smile. "You already have."

Chapter 6

The next morning, sitting in his office suite at the Fulton Foods corporate office in downtown Memphis, Eliot considered everything he'd seen and learned about the Mayfield Bakery the day before. And most important, what he'd learned about Sophie Mayfield.

After she'd settled into her new living space, the afternoon had pretty much taken off at twice the speed of the morning. She was like a general directing troops. As he watched her throughout the day, she coordinated delivery schedules for the weeks to come, assigning task and duties.

Eliot was surprised to learn that in addition to the few contracts she'd stolen from him, she had been busy getting other large contracts, as well.

His first order of business this morning had been to call his lawyer, Steve, and have him make another offer to purchase Mayfield. Now knowing what he knew, Eliot was certain he could custom-design a package that pretty little Sophie would find irresistible.

The door to his office swung open and slammed against the wall. Eliot sighed. He knew that eventually he was going to have to have that wall repaired and a stopper placed behind the door.

"Morning, Uncle Carl."

"Where were you yesterday?!"

Eliot sat back in his high-back leather chair, resting his elbows on the padded arms. "Out."

"Don't be coy with me, nephew! Where the hell were you? I tried calling you all afternoon and you didn't answer your cell phone."

Eliot narrowed his eyes on his uncle. "I haven't accounted for my whereabouts to you since I was twelve. So, what's this really about?"

"Got another damn e-mail!" He shook his fist and Eliot saw the crumpled papers for the first time.

He took the pages and pretended to be interested in what he was reading. He already knew it was for the Willows Day Care. He'd seen the requisition for their order yesterday. He considered warning his uncle that there would be one coming from the Thumbelina Nursery, as well, but decided that was only asking for trouble.

"Here we are sinking, and you're out gallivanting around."

"I told you I'm taking care of it."

"How? By spending the day doing whatever the hell you do, instead of finding a way to get rid of this little pain in my ass!"

Eliot picked up his pen and twirled it between his index fingers. "What if I told you I spent the day working in the kitchen of the Mayfield Bakery and now know a lot more about them than I did two days ago?"

For one of maybe three times in his life, Eliot realized he'd managed to surprise Carl.

"What?"

"I went there to speak to the owner. They all assumed I was the new baker, so I played along to get the feel of the place. Do you realize they are still using a recipe book?" He shook his head, still stunned by that fact. "The owner is a woman named Mae Ann Mayfield, but the real brains of the operation is the grand-daughter, Sophie. She's the real threat."

"How big an operation is it?"

"It's just what we thought it was—a small-town bakery. But I could see they were improving their equipment and processes, and with Sophie in charge they will be able to really compete soon enough."

"They are already competing, that's the problem. But…you were inside the store, huh?"

Eliot nodded slowly, not liking the look in his uncle's eyes one bit.

"Did they discover who you were?"

"No," he answered softly, knowing he was about to regret having said anything to Carl.

"You have to go back there and get that book."

"I can't." Eliot was a little spooked by the fact that his uncle had automatically come up with exactly the same idea he'd originally had.

"Why not? You said they didn't figure out who you were. Did you officially quit or just leave?"

Say you quit. Say you quit.

"I just left." Truth be told, Eliot himself wasn't sure why he didn't quit. That would've been the best way to close any loose ends and have no additional questions asked.

"Well, there! You see?"

"Uncle Carl, I will not—"

"Yes! You will." Carl leaned forward, bracing his hands on the desk. "Take as much time as you need. Move in if you have to, but get that book."

"Why this desire for their recipe book? Yesterday all you wanted was to put them out of business."

Carl stood straight. "That was before I actually tasted their product. I was out at Centerfield yesterday to talk to the head-mistress and try to get the contract back. She let me sample one of their pastries."

"And?"

"*And* it was damn good!" he snapped.

"Why not just let me deal with it my way, through negotiation? I'm sure we can come to some kind of an agreement with them."

"Why should we, when we've got an inside man? You can just stroll out the door with the recipe book."

Eliot could only imagine what his uncle would say if he knew he'd had that opportunity already and passed it up. "I don't know, Uncle Carl." He thought, refusing to admit how appealing the idea of seeing Sophie again really was. "The first time was a fluke, and I got away with it. But this time…if I'm caught, we are opening ourselves up to all kinds of legal repercussions."

His uncle's eyes narrowed in a familiar way. "Not if you do it right."

Eliot steepled his fingers on the desk. "You're asking me to *steal* from these people."

A nasty grin came across Carl's face. "Like you haven't thought of it already. Don't play with me, boy. I know you too well." He huffed. "I'm just surprised you haven't done it already."

Eliot felt the slight trace of shame wash over him at the truth of the words. "I'll think about it," he said, eager to be rid of his uncle.

"No, you'll do it. If you ever expect to sit in my chair, you'd better grow a pair and be prepared to do what must be done." Carl turned and started to leave. "I expect updated reports of your progress."

When Eliot was alone again, he turned to look out the glass window overlooking downtown Memphis. His stomach twisted in knots as he considered how low he was willing to go to sit in his uncle's chair.

Carl knew how to get to him. He'd always known. Everything from the most effective ways to punishment a sensitive boy to all the many evil ways to tempt a man. Carl knew the most coveted prize in his possession, as far as his nephew was concerned, was control of Fulton Foods.

It was the goal Eliot had spent his whole life working toward. Every aspect of his life had been built around the expectation that one day his uncle would turn over the reins. In his mind, it was the perfect vindication for the childhood he'd lost the day he moved into his uncle's home.

He'd always thought of himself in two parts. Just as history was divided in two parts—B.C. and A.D—his memories were divided into life Before Memphis and After Memphis.

And until today he'd held the Before Memphis part of himself well under control. But something about that small-town bakery and the people there called to that young boy. He knew part of it was Mae and her warm and generous spirit. But part of it was Sophie and all the contradictions she presented.

She was a sharp-minded businesswoman, but she was still trusting enough to let a total stranger walk out the door with their recipe book. She was professional and a fully capable manager, but the woman in her had instantly responded to the man in him. She made him think of what he could have been if he'd continued to be raised by his loving parents.

But despite the way he felt when he was with her, Sophie Mayfield and her bakery were nothing more than a bump in the road on his way to the top. That was all he could allow her to be. He'd worked too long and hard to turn back now.

As much as he hated to admit it, Carl was right. If he ever intended to run Fulton one day, he would have to learn to do things that at the time might seem unpalatable. As the old expression went, *You can't make an omelet without breaking a few eggs.*

After careful consideration, he made his decision. Eliot picked up the phone and called the agency.

After a few minutes of conversation with Tom, he understood why the real Alberto Montagna had not shown up yesterday. Apparently Sophie wasn't the only one in the hospital.

Alberto had been caught once again by the husband of his lover, and this time the man had tried to finish what he'd started before. Alberto was in critical condition. Eliot knew he should feel some sympathy for the man, but all he could feel was repulsion for his stupidity.

"Okay, Tom, thanks for the update. I would still like to offer him a position, so when he recovers please contact me. And for your assistance, I would like to pay you whatever you would have made from the Mayfield commission plus ten percent. How does that sound?"

Eliot smiled to himself as Tom eagerly accepted the offer. Wise man that he was, Tom didn't ask any uncomfortable questions about why a representative of Fulton was trying to steal a baker from a much smaller shop. Nor did he ask why Eliot did not want him contacting Mayfield directly anymore.

Later that afternoon, Eliot received a call from Steve and finally got all the dirt and history on Sophie Mayfield. The third and oldest daughter of Barbara Mayfield-Reynolds, she was born Sophia Riana Reynolds, and was a bit of a family black sheep. In honor of the grandparents she adored, Sophie had taken her mother's maiden name when she was eighteen, much to her father's fury.

By some strange twist of fate, Mae and Earl Mayfield, the adventurous family icons, had produced a family of ultraconservatives. With the exception of the eldest daughter, Sharyn, all their children—Kevin, Tobias, Barbara and Tina—were married and in stable relationships. Among the five, they'd produced twelve grandchildren. Two of them—Sophie and Lonnie—were close to their maternal grandmother; the others had all moved away.

Apparently, a few years ago, shortly after Sophie had graduated from college, where she majored in marketing, the family pushed Mae to sell the bakery and move into an assisted-living facility. Sophie and Mae had pushed back and won. Sophie had turned down a lucrative offer to work for a large marketing firm in New York, choosing instead to stay in Selmer and help her grandmother run the bakery. That move had apparently been enough for her parents to call it quits and break ties with her.

And the rest he'd pretty much witnessed yesterday. The bakery had never really taken off the way the pair had hoped, and were still hoping. But Sophie was still completely dedicated to her grandmother, and after meeting Mae, Eliot understood why.

He and Steve discussed the new offer for Mayfield, then he left for the day to do some shopping. If he was going to be a baker for however long, he would have to look like one. He couldn't afford to keep going through four-hundred-dollar suits.

If he'd been an outside observer, Eliot realized he would have had nothing but respect and admiration for Sophie and her grandmother. Going up against Fulton, they were truly a modern day "David and Goliath" story.

But, he wasn't an outside observer; he was the heir to the Fulton Food conglomerate. But heir or not, if he wanted the seat at the top of the heap, he would have to earn it. Even if it came through deceit and dishonest means. As beautifully inspirational as the original biblical story was, Eliot thought, this time…David would lose the battle.

Chapter 7

The next day, Eliot was back at work in the bakery. He tried not to think too closely about how good and natural it felt to be there, despite the discomfort of working in a kitchen on a hot June morning.

He'd been welcomed back warmly, and no one seemed to suspect anything out of the ordinary. It was a little awkward at first because Sophie insisted on directing his efforts from her wheelchair. Eliot had never been responsive to being micromanaged. Even as an underling in his uncle's factory he'd resented it, and he certainly wasn't responsive to it now years later and at a much higher pay grade. It didn't help that he hadn't actually done any serious baking in years. His skills were rusty. He needed some time and a couple of practice batches of dough to get a feel for it again. But that was next to impossible with Sophie watching his every move.

After about an hour and a half, he wiped his hands on his apron and squatted down next to her chair. "Sophie, what's going on?"

"What do you mean?"

"Why are you riding me like this? Did I do something to make you think I'm incompetent?"

"No! of course not!"

"Then why are you watching me like a kid fresh out of culinary school?"

Her wide brown eyes watched his for a few moments, and then she burst into laughter. "Boredom."

"What?"

She exploded in frustration. "This chair is driving me crazy! I can't go everywhere I want to, or do everything I want to. I read through all my magazines by ten last night and still couldn't sleep. I just laid there staring at the ceiling. Wayne is out gassing up and washing the delivery truck, and I have no idea where Lonnie and Dante are, and Grandma is up front with a customer. But, you're here."

Eliot hid a smile. Her frustrations were real, but it was such a relief to realize it wasn't what he'd feared: that she'd somehow discovered the truth. "So that's it? You're just bored?"

"I'm freakin bored out of my mind!" She laughed again. "And unfortunately, you work in the kitchen, so I guess I've kinda leeched on to you."

Eliot stood again. "Tell you what." He walked over to the mixer and pulled out a blob of dough. Bringing it back he flopped it down on the table in front of her. "If you want to work, I'll put you to work."

He pushed her up to the table, then reaching into the large bowl that took up half the table, he sprinkled some flour on the blob.

"What am I suppose to do with that?" she asked, eyeing the blob warily.

"Make a pie crust out of it."

She glared up at him. "If I could do that I wouldn't have hired you."

"My, my, my, how the tide changes. As long as you were sitting there doling out orders like a little dictator you were happy. I actually try to get you to do some work, and suddenly you're all attitude."

She chuckled. "Fine." Eliot watched her reach for the blob as if afraid it would bite her at any minute.

Eliot returned to his task of making crescent rolls. He only hoped they came out even and crusty.

A minute later, he looked over and she was still pulling hesitantly at the blob. With a soft laugh, he came up behind the wheelchair. "Here, like this." Covering her hands, he squeezed the soft dough, feeling it mesh through their combined fingers. "Don't be afraid of it. Think of it like modeling clay."

"But I never planned to eat it."

"Then you missed out. Yum."

She laughed, as he hoped she would. "You're not serious? You didn't actually eat clay?"

"I sure did. But in my defense I was only four or five. At that age, all kinds of things taste good."

"You could've been sick."

"Nah, why do you think toys go through so much testing? They're all eatable, really. The scientists make sure if any of it accidentally goes in one end, it comes out the other."

"Ugh, we are baking here!"

"Sorry." He smiled, enjoying the feeling of their combined fingers squeezing the bread. "See how it's starting to take shape?"

She glanced down at their hands together, the lighter color of his against the deeper brown of hers. She liked the way it looked…too much.

His hands were smooth—unlike Wayne's, whose hands had rough calluses. Which reminded her of the differences in the two men. She wondered if El had ever done a hard day's work in his life. Although she had to admit that in his white T-shirt and jeans, he looked like any other workingman. The only sign of his wealth were his expensive designer loafers.

He leaned closer, his soft musk cologne drifting into her nose. She tried to focus on the dough they were kneading, but her eyes drifted to his profile, as his face was right beside hers now. She looked up at the newly formed locks and could see his soft hair was resisting the style.

She watched with a dry mouth as he leaned forward to collect more flour from the big bowl, his bicep stretching with the motion. *When did they start building bakers like this?* she thought.

Pounding the dough with more flour, he wrapped his hands around hers again and continue to knead. "See? You're getting the hang of it…that's it."

Sophie tried to focus on the dough and not the man behind her. Beside her. Surrounding her.

"Push…pull, and turn." His soft breath moved the hairs closest to her ear. "There you go." He spoke like a patient coach, and she wanted to form something wonderful out of the dough just to satisfy him.

"See, I knew you could do it." He turned and looked at her, bringing their lips within inches of each other. His minty breath was warm, and she found herself licking dry lips, which brought his eyes straight to her mouth, which made her mouth dry again.

They continued to stare at each other; neither seemed able to look away. Unable to stop herself, she licked her dry lips again, and it seemed to be some kind of a signal to him, because he leaned forward and gently touched his lips to hers.

Sophie released a sigh of relief, as if she'd been waiting for that soft kiss her whole life. He pulled back a little to look in her eyes and apparently he saw what he was looking for because he kissed her again and this time more deeply.

His mouth opening over hers, their lips meshed and tongues swirled together. Sophie reached up, wrapping her arms around his head, and he came to her. Kneeling beside the chair, he took her face between his hands and deepened the kiss.

The noise of people coming into the kitchen startled both of them, and they quickly broke apart. Eliot stood and returned to his place by the table, once again forming crescent rolls.

Sophie poked and prodded at the blob Eliot had given her, still not completely sure what to do with it.

Both of them thought they'd done a good job of giving no sign of the kiss they'd shared. Neither realizing that the flour fingerprints they'd left all over each other's face and hands served as a road map to any curious onlookers, like the two who had just walked by.

That Saturday Sophie had scheduled two weddings. She had been contracted to cater two weddings that weekend, and the orders were so large she'd decided to lock up the front of the store so that everyone could work on the wedding cakes and assorted desserts. What they would make from the two weddings would more than compensate for any loss from walk-in business.

By the afternoon, the kitchen was like a boiler room, and Wayne had propped the back door open to let in some air.

Sophie scooted around the area, trying to do her part and stay out of everyone's way at the same time. But they needed every hand they could get. Even Lonnie was helping out where she could.

Eliot was completely engrossed in his task, showing Mae some complicated twist design, flipping and turning dough and filling multiple trays with bread, but leaving the actual baking to Wayne. Dante was gently packing up box after box of desserts, using boxes Lonnie built.

Once Eliot was confident Mae understood what he wanted, he moved across the room to finish decorating a tray of tarts, then truffles. The preparation tables were already filled with trays of cookies, minicakes and little chocolate mousse cups. And then there were the smaller cakes, which came in all varieties—tortes covered in rich, dark chocolate with sweet strawberry topping dripping over the sides, gateau with hazelnuts and a cinnamon chocolate mixture, pavlova with sweet marshmallow centers topped with assorted berries, and little banana and chocolate soufflés. Sophie had never seen such a varied collection of delectable foods in her kitchen. She was surprised by El's eye for design. It was understated and elegant. Then again there were a lot of things about him that Sophie found surprising.

The twin towered wedding cakes were already packed in portions to be put together on arrival at the receptions. They were given a preparation table in the far corner, out of the way of traffic.

She watched as sweat rolled over his sinewy biceps as he worked tirelessly, moving from one task to the next. His white T-shirt clung to his copper skin. Everything about him was divinely masculine, and yet his glove-covered fingers moved over the delicate desserts like a surgeon at work. Sophie realized she could have contently spent the evening watching him work.

A little after six, the van pulled away from the bakery loaded down with boxes of desserts. Wayne, Lonnie and Dante squeezed into the front seat. While Eliot and Mae stood on the sidewalk, watching them pull away, Sophie sat in her chair just inside the door, wishing she were able to go with them to double-check the setups.

Once the van was out of sight, El held the door open as Mae reentered the store. She smiled up at him and laughed. "It's been a long time since we've hustled like that."

Sophie noticed how bright and cheery her grandmother's face was, considering the day they'd had. She looked as bright and eager as a schoolgirl. *Maybe the activity is good for her,* Sophie thought.

Feeling El's eyes on her, Sophie looked up at him. "I really appreciated what you did today," she said. "I don't know how we could've done it without you."

"Just doing my job," he said, but it sounded more regretful than anything. And he just continued to watch her in that unsettling way of his. "I'm going to go out back and get some air." He wiped his hand over his face before passing between the two women heading toward the kitchen.

"That's a good man, and a fine baker," Mae said with a satisfied nod. "When you first told us you'd hired a new baker, I didn't know what to think. I was a little hurt at first. But the truth is, I could never have gotten out those orders today. Not like he did."

Sophie just listened. The reasons Mae had just named were indeed a part of her decision to hire the extra help, but she wouldn't insult her grandmother by acknowledging it.

"I'm going to head on home," Mae said. "I'm starting to get a little tired, and tonight my show comes on."

Sophie smiled. "Ah, yes, supersleuth and mystery writer Jessica Fletcher. Doesn't it kinda bother you how she *always* happens to be nearby with someone is murdered?"

"Oh, hush." Mae laughed, moving behind the counter to get her purse. "I don't try to ruin your shows, so why are you trying to ruin mine?"

"Sorry," Sophie said with a laugh. "Didn't mean to spoil your fun." She glanced out the window, glad to see there was plenty of sunlight left, enough for her grandmother to get home safely.

Mae kissed her granddaughter on the forehead. "Love you, pumpkin. Don't forget to lock up the shop after El leaves."

"I won't. See you in the morning. Drive safely."

"Sophie…" Mae reached out and touched Sophie's cheek in that way she did when she had something important to say. "That's a good man." She nodded toward the back. "He's got some demons he's fighting, not sure what they are, but…you could do worse."

Sophie frowned, wondering where this had come from.

Mae only smiled. "I ain't so old I can't remember what love looks like."

Sophie was startled out of her confusion. "El? You think I'm in love with the new baker? I've only known him two days."

"I'm not trying to speak for your emotions." She shrugged. "Just saying, that kiss earlier didn't look like it was being shared by two strangers—that's all I'm saying."

Sophie was mortified from the top of her head to the tips of her toes, realizing her grandmother and Wayne had witnessed more that she'd thought. Deciding there was no use in denying it, she said, "I'll admit I'm attracted to him, but that's all. It's not love."

Mae only smiled in that knowing way of hers as she turned and headed out the door. "At least, not yet," she called back just as she went through the door.

Chapter 8

She glanced briefly at the tables where the second order sat waiting to be delivered in the next half an hour. The kitchen had been cleared and cleaned up, and they were ready for business the next day.

She rolled up to the back door and found El standing against the building. His hands rested at his sides and his eyes were closed, and for a moment she thought he might have fallen asleep.

"Mama Mae left?"

Sophie rolled a little closer, careful not to tip over the ledge and onto the concrete a few inches below. "Yes. She's a *Murder, She Wrote* junkie."

He smiled. "She's one sweet lady."

Sophie smiled herself. "Yes, she is."

Lifting her face, she let the breeze blow over her skin. Surprisingly the alley wasn't in the least bit smelly. The large containers at the end were where all the businesses in the little strip mall dumped their trash. But the city did a good job of emptying them regularly. Which was good, considering she shared the strip with a Chinese restaurant and a pet store. A video rental store and a dress shop rounded out the small shopping center.

"You can go on home if you want," she offered. Although she found his company comforting, she knew he had to be tired.

"I'm good. Just need a minute to wind down." He glanced at her, his amber eyes running over her quickly. "How are you doing?"

"Me?" she asked with a chuckle. "I've been sitting in a chair all day."

"Yeah, but I know stress and pressure can wear out the body as easily as physical labor."

"I'm fine." She considered saying something about the kiss they'd shared earlier, but then thought maybe it was best to leave it alone.

"I don't like you staying in this store alone at night."

She looked at him, surprised by the possessive tone of his voice. He spoke like his opinion on the matter carried some weight. She could have told him it didn't, but instead said, "Once I lock up, it's as safe as anywhere else."

He sighed. "Still don't like it."

"It's not for you to like," she muttered, unable to hold back the remark. She closed her eyes briefly. When would she learn to control her flippant tongue? she wondered.

He glanced at her with a smile but did not say anything in response. She looked away quickly, slightly envious of his self-restraint.

"About earlier," he said. "I hope I wasn't out of line."

"What do you mean?"

"When I kissed you."

She laughed. "Funny, I thought *I* kissed *you*."

He frowned. "No, I'm pretty sure it was the other way around."

She shrugged. "If that's what you want to believe."

He turned toward her, leaning his hip against the wall. "That's what I want to believe because that's what happened."

"Oh…I get it." She smiled flirtatiously. "It's some kind of macho thing." Then she nodded sagely. "Okay, then—yeah, you're right, *you* kissed *me*."

He shook his head with a laugh. "You are something else, girl."

Sophie laughed with him, loving every bit of their flirtatious banter. It had been a long time since she'd played with a man like this. Most of her days were filled with work, and she spent her nights in an exhausted sleep as a result.

But last night, as she lay staring at the ceiling, El's image had passed before her eyes many times. There was so much about him that she didn't know, and every minute revealed things that didn't fit. For instance, there was no way she could see this man working in the kitchen of the exclusive and very posh Catalan's. Yet he seemed surprisingly at home in her kitchen. And it wasn't that he lacked sophistication. It's just that his polish seemed more along the lines of someone who'd worked his way up from modest beginning to a cultured lifestyle, not someone who served those who did. Sophie had learned a lot about both types of people when she left the small town of Selmer to go to Duke.

On the large campus, she'd met every type of personality imaginable, and in her opinion El fit too well in her world to have come from anywhere else. She wondered about his background, the man he was before culinary school.

"So?"

Sophie was startled out of her reverie as she realized he'd crossed in front of her and was currently speaking to her. "So?"

He pulled back and gave her a curious look. "Where were you?"

She smiled. "Sorry, my mind's running at a million miles an hour. What did you say?"

"I said—" he leaned forward, bracing his hands on the arms of her wheelchair "—there is one way to settle the matter of who kissed who."

She felt her heart rate begin to speed up as she anticipated the kiss to come. "Oh?" She licked her dry lips, and he shook his head once before swooping down on her mouth.

Sophie eagerly welcomed him, wrapping her arms around his neck. She gasped against his open mouth as he lifted her up out of the chair. He cradled her in his arms as his mouth devoured hers.

His taste was sweet and minty, his full lips delectable. So much so, she couldn't resist gently clamping her teeth down on his bottom lip.

His head came up, and his eyes twinkled with mischief. "Hmm, didn't peg you as a biter."

She tightened her arms around his neck, bringing his lips back down to hers. She didn't want to talk or flirt; she wanted his mouth against hers. His hands on her body, his body over hers. Her whole being tingled with the images conjured by her mind. The feeling of his warm copper flesh against hers. Suddenly there were too many clothes between them, as his soft lips traced the veins of her neck, up behind her ear and sent a shiver through her.

"I want you," she whispered against his chest, running her tongue over his salty shoulder, feeling the muscles just beneath the skin.

"That's all I needed to hear." Using his foot, El pushed the chair back out of the doorway as he stepped up into the kitchen, still holding her cradled in his arms.

He turned toward her back bedroom, then froze as they both heard the chime on the front door ring. Lonnie's noisy chatter drifted into the kitchen, followed by Dante's quiet response.

Sophie looked at the man holding her tightly against his chest and saw her disappointment reflected in his brown eyes. She smiled. "I should've locked the front door."

He smiled back. "It wouldn't have made a difference."

She sighed in frustration. "You're right. Wayne has a key."

El bent his head and kissed her lips once more, a soft touch, and a promise. Then gently sat her back down in her chair, and whispered in her ear, "We'll get our chance to be together, just not tonight."

She looked up at him, unable to hide her desire. "You promise?"

He nodded with pure determination. "Absolutely."

"Well?"

"Well, what?" Eliot turned from the open door of his condo as Carl entered.

"How is it going? Find out anything interesting? Who do they plan to bid on next? What shape are their finances in? I wish I were a little younger and less known, I'd do this myself. I know how to get the information we need."

Eliot stretched his tired body, ignoring the old man's tirade. He worked out regularly, but even that could not prepare him for the rigors of life in a small, family-owned bakery.

Fulton used nothing but the latest technology and equipment, and the staff was so large, no one man was stuck doing manual labor for any length of time. But Eliot was quickly learning Mayfield was no place for a spoiled, pampered baker—or executive. Alberto Montagna wouldn't have lasted a day.

And now, his uncle was here giving him the third degree, and all he wanted was a hot shower and his bed. He slumped down on his chenille sofa. "This was your idea, not mine."

Carl lifted an eyebrow, and Eliot felt as if he were getting a glimpse of his own face in forty years. "Wasn't it? As I recall, you started this before I found out about it."

He sighed. "No, nothing interesting has come up. I've only been there a week. And Wayne watches me like a stalker."

"Who's Wayne?"

"One of the employees. He doesn't trust me."

"Why?"

Eliot chuckled. "Good instincts."

"Well, find a way around him. This can't go on too long. I need you back at the office."

"Why are you so determined to get this book?"

"I've tasted their product. It's excellent." Carl sat down in a nearby side chair. "They could do it, Eliot."

"Do what?"

"Challenge us—seriously challenge us. If we don't stop them now, we may never have another opportunity."

"You make it sound like they are some ruthless corporate raiders trying to bring you down. They're just a nice family trying to make a living wage."

Carl's eyes narrowed on his nephew's face. "Are you getting attached to these people, Eliot?"

"No," he lied.

"Good, because I wouldn't recommend it. Caring only clutters things." Carl nodded emphatically. "I want that recipe book *and*

I want them out of business. And I want it done quickly." As he started to leave the condo, Carl called back over his shoulder. "And get a shower. You smell like a horse."

As soon as he locked the door behind his uncle, Eliot did just that. Standing under the hot spray, his mind wandered back to the day he'd spent in the bakery and a world so far from the life he lived in Memphis as a marketing executive. In fact, he felt like he was really living two lives, and he was having a harder and harder time telling which was real.

At the Mayfield Bakery everyone was treated as family, and the whole feel of the place was warm and well lived in. Eliot had become an accepted part of that group. Of course, Wayne still watched him, but he was pretty sure that had more to do with Wayne's feelings for Sophie than any real suspicion on his part.

He soaped his body, thinking about Sophie. She was amazing, scooting around the shop in that wheelchair like a little rolling dynamo. He could only imagine what she was like without the encumbrance of the chair.

True to her word, she spent her nights at the store, sleeping in the back room. The idea made him uncomfortable, but being practically a stranger he, of course, had no say-so in the matter.

He'd caught a glimpse of the back rooms a couple of times. All they contained was a small bathroom with a standing shower, sink and toilet, and a small bedroom where she kept a twin bed and a small television. A few books and magazines were stacked next to the bed.

She was young, but it was obvious she'd been running the store in place of her grandmother for some time. He often wondered where the rest of their family was. Other than Lonnie, there was no one else around. That was odd. Usually with family-run businesses, the whole family got in on the act.

Sophie was smart and had the foresight of a fortune-teller. They never ran too low on anything. Customers never had to wait too long to be served. And what he liked most about her was her eye for marketing. She knew how to promote her goods. Eliot had thought more than once that he could use someone with Sophie's natural ability at Fulton. Not to mention the fact that she kissed like an angel.

She was the most surprising thing about the whole Mayfield story, he thought. He quickly rinsed his body and climbed out of the shower, anticipating the next day. As exhausted as he was, Eliot found that he was actually enjoying his time with these people. They reminded him of the friends and neighbors of his childhood. There was a realness to them, an authentic way of behaving that let you know right away whom you were dealing with.

The world he'd encountered when he moved into his uncle's house was completely foreign to him. It took him years to learn that some people lied for no apparent reason. That deceit was the expectation, and now, all these years later, he'd become an expert in that world.

The proof was in how he was able to go into that bakery, look that sweet old lady in the face and lie without compunction. But, that wasn't exactly true anymore.

It was getting harder and harder to maintain the façade, and he found himself slipping more and more often. Showing more and more of himself. As if in the face of such sincerity, he had no choice but to offer the same.

The following Saturday morning, Eliot caught the earliest flight to Houston, and by noon he was walking into the hospital room of Alberto Montagna. According to the agency, Alberto had regained consciousness two days ago. Eliot found him sitting up in the bed, his badly battered face partially bandaged.

Seeing he had a visitor, he turned his television to mute. "Hello?"

Eliot came forward and introduced himself. "Mr. Montagna, my name is Eliot Wright. I believe the agency may have told you I was coming?"

He nodded slightly. "Yes, Mr. Wright. I can't thank you enough for your generous offer—" he gestured down at his body "—but as you can see, I am in no condition to come work for you."

"I understand that," Eliot said, and handed the injured man his card. "But when you can, call me at this number. Call me directly."

He grabbed a pen from the nightstand and scribbled an offer amount on the back. "Whenever you are ready, I will honor that."

Alberto took the card and read the amount. His one good eye opened wide. "Seriously?"

"Seriously. But I do have to ask two things in return. Things that you can do for me today."

"What is that?"

"One, make no attempt to contact Mayfield Bakery. They are a competitor of ours, and we would prefer you not communicate with them."

Alberto nodded his agreement.

"Second, I would like to do a brief interview with you, learn a little about you and your background. Your résumé speaks for itself." He smiled. "But I would like to get to know a little about the man, not the chef. Is that okay?"

Alberto nodded once more, and Eliot pulled up a chair. He pulled the list of questions he'd prepared from his jacket pocket. They were very specific questions, things he needed to know in order to continue impersonating the man.

Chapter 9

Eliot was starting to realize he had a shadow. Wherever he turned, Lonnie would be there watching him intently with her large doe eyes. He'd smile. She'd smile back. And he would walk away, only to be ambushed again a few minutes later.

He was forming loaves of cinnamon-flavored bread that afternoon, when she finally worked up the nerve to speak to him. Even after the mixer was done with the dough, Eliot always took the time to knead it with his hands the way his mother taught him. He'd learned working in the factory that the mixer wasn't always as thorough as it should be. And there was nothing less tasty than dough with an uneven amount of yeast and cinnamon.

"How long you been a baker?" she asked, standing on the other side of the table, nibbling on an elephant-ear pastry.

"All my life." Eliot felt that was at least partially true.

"You're very good at it." She smiled in a way that made him a little uncomfortable. It wasn't the usual casual smile she gave him. This one had purpose.

"Thank you." He glanced around the empty kitchen, wondering where Dante was. The boy always seemed to be no more than two steps behind her. He decided to ask. "So, where's Dante?"

"I don't know." She shrugged. "You got a girlfriend?"

The uncomfortably feeling grew even stronger. He glanced around again, and saw Sophie had rolled out of the office. Heading toward the front of the store, but hearing Lonnie's question she'd paused.

Eliot glanced in her direction and they briefly made eye contact as he smiled and said, "Not at the moment."

Sophie looked away and quickly rolled her chair to the front of the store. Eliot was so busy watching Sophie, it took him a moment to realize Lonnie's expression had changed, as well. Suddenly, her eyes seemed clearer, more focused—on him.

"Why not?" she asked, tossing the last bit of elephant ear in her mouth and dusting the crumbs from her fingers.

Eliot shrugged, wondering how to get her off this subject. "What about you?"

She smiled shyly. "No, I don't have a boyfriend." She looked up at him, and Eliot was suddenly *extremely* uncomfortable. Mentally challenged or not, this was a young woman fully aware of her sexuality and the art of seduction. He wondered if Sophie, who was so protective of the girl, was aware of just how much her little cousin really knew.

As if he'd been summoned, Dante appeared in the doorway. "Lonnie, I'm going down to make a delivery at Montgomery High. Wanna come?"

"No thanks," she answered, never taking her eyes off Eliot.

Dante threw a quick glare at Eliot, but Eliot pretended not to see it while continuing to knead the bread. He wanted Lonnie gone from him as much as Dante did. The last thing he needed was Sophie's little cousin coming on to him.

"Why not?" Dante was asking, as he walked closer. "You always come with me, and we always go to the park afterwards."

She glanced over her shoulder at him. "Not today. Maybe next time."

As Sophie came back into the kitchen, Dante said, "Sophie, I need Lonnie's help with the Montgomery delivery—is that okay?"

Lonnie's attention snapped to Dante, and she practically snarled, "I said no!"

Sophie smiled, seemingly completely oblivious to the undercurrent of emotions. "Why not, Lonnie? It's a beautiful day out. I kinda wish I was doing the deliveries," she said.

Lonnie's eyes darted back and forth. She was obviously torn. She couldn't exactly explain that she wanted to stay and continue to flirt with the new baker, and she didn't have any legitimate reason for not going. Eliot watched the slow smile come across Dante's face, realizing he'd won.

She huffed. "Fine." She turned and, moving quickly around Dante, headed out of the kitchen. Dante followed at a slower pace.

Sophie frowned at the pair. "Wonder what's got into her?" She looked at El, expecting an answer.

And he shrugged, trying to look clueless. Sophie turned and rolled her chair back into the office.

As he loaded the metal baking sheet with the long loaves of bread, Eliot replayed the entire incident in his head, and finally concluded that things were not what they appeared with Lonnie Mayfield. *Mentally challenged, my ass,* he thought, sliding the tray into the oven.

An hour later, he and Wayne were once again kneeling before the older oven, trying to get it going. Eliot was showing the other man how to push the coils back into place for a temporary fix. This was the fifth time it had stopped working in the past two weeks.

"So, where did you work before you came here?" Wayne asked, trying to sound casually interested. Eliot wasn't fooled.

He'd expected this interrogation eventually, he was only unsure as to why it took so long. He gave Wayne the brief history he'd learned from Alberto like the well-rehearsed lie it was, ending with his employment at Catalan's in Houston.

Wayne seemed to accept the story, but Eliot knew it was not the last time his past would come up. This man would love nothing better than to find a reason to get rid of him.

"Catalan's?" Wayne asked, recognizing the name of the five-star restaurant. "How the hell you end up here?"

"Wayne!" Sophie snapped, rolling up to the pair.

Kneeling by the oven, Eliot found himself right at eye level with her as she came to a stop beside him. For a moment their eyes met, and he wished they were alone. But Wayne was right on the other side of him, as always, watching him closely. And Mae was just across the room, vacuuming up a busted bag of flour.

There were always too many people around as far as Eliot was concerned. Far too many people for him to attempt to explore whatever this was, this something that seemed to be happening between them. He'd known she was attracted to him from the moment he met her, but she'd tucked away that initial desire. He'd not seen that look in her eyes again in the past few weeks, until lately.

She seemed to have come to a decision. She'd been allowing him to look closer, to look into her again, and he found that was all he wanted to do. Like now or anytime she was near. She was all he could think about. The air in the room would thicken with unspoken thoughts.

"How he came to be here is none of your business—or mine, for that matter. Did you get the oven fixed?"

"Yes, temporarily, but you need to call a professional, Sophie. This temporary fix can only last so long," Wayne said.

"I know." She bit her lip. "But we just can't afford it right now."

"I thought business was good," Eliot said, closing the oven door. "I mean with all the new contracts."

"It's getting better, but we have a long way to go before it can be categorized as good."

"Hmm."

"Oh, but don't worry, we are stable," she quickly added, mistaking his grunt for concern.

Over the past weeks Eliot was beginning to understand why his generous buyout offer had been rejected. For Sophie and Mae it wasn't about the money. They needed the money to grow the business, but it was the legacy of the business that mattered most to them. How was he supposed to talk them into selling when all he could offer was money? That approach would never work.

Wayne had stood and turned on the oven. Pressing his hand

against the glass window, he nodded, satisfied. "That will hold it for a while."

Mae finished her vacuuming and began rewrapping the cord. "I don't know what we would've done without you these past weeks, El," she called over her shoulder.

"Here, Mama Mae, let me get that for you." Wayne crossed the room and lifted the heavy vacuum to carry it out to the shed across the alley, where they kept overflow supplies, broken kitchen equipment and various other things.

"Wayne, when you're done with that can you run me down to the hospital for my checkup?" Sophie called.

"I can take you," Eliot offered.

Wayne almost dropped the vacuum on his foot. "I'll take her," he said quickly.

Sophie was looking up at Eliot. "No, Wayne, it's fine. El can take me." She smiled. "Thanks for the offer."

He smiled back. "No problem." Finally, they'd have a chance to be alone.

A few minutes later, El lifted Sophie out of her wheelchair, enjoying every second of holding her small body against his. He wrapped one arm around her back, the other under her knees, and took his time sitting her down in the bucket seat of his champagne-colored sports car. He was careful not to bump her cast.

She glanced up at him with those sparkling brown eyes that revealed much of what she was thinking. "Thank you."

"No, thank you." He grinned playfully.

"Nice car," she said, as he climbed in beside her.

"Thanks. Now, where are we going?"

"I really appreciate this." She dug around in her purse and came up with her doctor's business card.

Glancing at the address, he started the car and began to back up. "I meant it when I said no problem. Besides, like you told Lonnie, it really is too nice a day to be inside."

She rested her arm on the console between them, glancing over the controls. "I'm sorry about Wayne's rude question." She looked at him and quickly looked away. "I guess I should warn you that I know about your circumstances."

He frowned. "My circumstances?"

"You know…how you came to be no longer employed at Catalan's."

"Oh, right." He nodded, remembering that she thought he was someone else. He couldn't afford to forget that.

"But I meant what I said. It's not Wayne's business or mine."

"Right, well, we all make mistakes."

She snorted quietly. "A mistake."

As he pulled out of the parking lot he opened the sunroof and asked, "What's that supposed to mean?"

"Nothing." She looked at him with wide, innocent brown eyes. "I just don't know if I would call sleeping with a powerful man's *wife* a mistake."

"Mistake, indiscretion, whatever word works for you." He didn't like the judgmental tone he was hearing in her voice. Even though he was not the one who'd actually done the deed, she was sounding a little too prudish for his taste.

"Do you do that often?"

"What?"

"Sleep with other men's wives."

Eliot smiled to himself. Maybe that wasn't judgment he was hearing but jealousy. "Depends on the woman." He looked directly at her. "I find some women are simply irresistible."

"Was she worth it?"

Eliot considered his life, his ambitions and dreams for the future. Would he be willing to sacrifice all he'd built in life for one night with another man's wife? "No." He shifted gears and changed lanes as he merged onto the freeway. "Can we talk about something else?"

"Like what?"

"Like what's between you and Wayne?"

"Friendship, a great working relationship and trust."

"Nothing more?"

"That's none of your business," she answered coyly.

"Oh, I get it. You get *all up in* my business, all the while talking about how it's *none* of your business. But when I ask a question, you throw that back in my face." He laughed, and she laughed with him, realizing he was right. "I answered your questions. It's only fair you answer mine."

She sighed. "No, there's nothing more between us."

"You sound disappointed."

She shrugged. "He's a good man, just not the one for me."

"How can you be so sure?"

"I'll know when I meet Mr. Right." She nodded.

Eliot *Wright* almost laughed out loud. "Sure you will."

"What? You don't believe me?"

"What are we talking about here? Love at first sight?"

"Something like that."

"Then no, I don't believe you. You can't love someone you know nothing about."

"Maybe not love at first sight, but there's a feeling you get when you meet someone you know could be special in your life. Know what I mean?"

"Yep. It's called lust, and it keeps a lot of divorce attorneys in business."

"No, not lust, and not love. It's something in between. I can't put a name to it."

He chuckled. "When you do, please let me know what this mysterious something in between is."

She tilted her head, watching him warily. "Are you always this cynical?"

He almost answered yes but bit his tongue. He hadn't always been, but twenty years with Carl Fulton had removed any traces of the optimistic boy he'd once been. "Sorry, it's just been a rough few months."

"I'm sure," she said, sympathetically. "Someone with your obvious talent being forced to work for a small bakery in a backwater town. I'm a little surprised you took the offer."

"I didn't have much of a choice," he answered, thinking of his uncle and knowing she would believe he meant something different.

"So why don't you have a girlfriend or a wife of your own?"

He put on his signal and got over preparing to exit the freeway. "Back to my love life again?"

"Sorry." But she didn't really sound it.

Eliot just laughed and shook his head. He was enjoying her company, even if she seemed to have a one-track mind. Truth was, he didn't mind the track it was on. Not one bit.

Chapter 10

A month later, Eliot was stuffing a tray of donuts with filling, but his mind was still on his last conversation with his uncle. Carl was getting more and more demanding. And Eliot was feeling more and more like Judas.

He glanced at Mae at her stove in the far corner, where she spent most of her time preparing meals for them. For him. Every day, she fed them lunches fit for a king, and he'd look into her soft brown eyes and smile.

Then there was Sophie, who watched him with intensity when she thought no one was watching her. He knew she was attracted to him—if nothing else, the one kiss they'd shared proved that. But she was always careful to keep their relationship on the level.

Dante and Lonnie accepted him without question, and even Wayne seemed to have begrudgingly accepted him. But the guilt of living a double life was starting to get to him, and he wasn't sure how much more he could take.

Sophie rolled up beside him. "El? Can I ask you for a favor?" She lifted a key on a ring. "Wayne is off today, and Dante's out doing deliveries. So can you run out to the shed and bring in twenty cans of peach filling?"

He wiped his hands on his apron. "No problem." As he took the key, their hands touched briefly, and Sophie snatched her hand back as if scorched by fire. "You okay?"

She nodded and began rolling away.

Eliot quickly brought in the large cans of peach filling, stacking them on an empty preparation table. By then Sophie had rolled into the large pantry area. She sat with a clipboard on her lap, counting cans and boxes on the shelf.

He leaned against the door and watched her work, then she turned to leave and saw him. She was so startled she almost bounced right up out of her chair.

"Sorry." He smiled. "Didn't mean to scare you." He handed the key over. "Here you go."

She waved it away. "You might as well keep it. It's a spare, and I'm sure you'll need it again." He glanced at the key with interest for the first time and realized there were two keys on the chain. "What's this other one for?"

"The store. It opens the front and back doors. Just make sure you don't lose it," she said.

"Sophie, is everything okay?"

"Yeah, why?"

"You just seem different."

"Different from what?"

He glanced over her shoulder. Mae was now in the front of the store and everyone else was out, so he felt comfortable speaking freely. "I kinda thought something was happening here." He gestured to himself and to her. "And now you won't even look me in the eyes."

She looked slightly startled. "Oh? You thought that little flirting meant something? I'm sorry, I was just playing around, you know...passing the time."

Eliot didn't believe that for a minute. "I see."

"I'm sorry if you misunderstood. But it's not like you're going to be here any length of time." She grinned playfully. "Just waiting for your lover's husband to cool off, right? You don't want to get into something with a one-legged woman in a back-woods town." She laughed as if tickled by her own comment. But Eliot could feel it was forced.

When he didn't laugh with her, Sophie cleared her throat. "Well, back to work." She pushed on past him and into her office.

Eliot stood for several minutes, staring down at the key in his hand. *She trusts me with the key to her store, but not to her heart,* he thought. His fingers closed around the key ring.

It only got worse from there. Wayne had caught a pretty bad summer cold, which knocked him out of commission for a few days. During that time, Sophie became more and more dependent on Eliot.

By the end of that week he'd helped Sophie complete the payroll and do inventory, and he fixed the broken coil on the old oven two times, in addition to his daily duties. But it wasn't until that Friday evening, when he found himself in his car on the way to the bank with the store's deposit, that it hit him just how much she'd come to trust him.

During that time, his last and best offer had arrived from Steve's office via courier. Eliot had made a point of going into the office to talk to Sophie just as she was opening the envelope. He wanted to gauge her reaction to the offer to see if they were even getting close to a number they could agree on.

Sophie quickly scanned the letter and the offer attached. Then, with a heavy sigh, she tossed both on the desk.

"Bad news?" Eliot asked, pretending to read through Mae's recipe book

"Oh, no." She smiled, but there was a sadness to it. "Very good news, actually."

"What do you mean?"

"It's an offer for the business."

"Are you going to take it?"

"No, I can't."

"Why not?"

She looked at him as if surprised by the question. "It's not mine to sell."

"Why not show the offer to Mama Mae, and get her opinion? She may surprise you and want to sell."

Sophie sighed. "She won't."

Realizing he was losing the battle, he moved forward. "Can I?" he asked. She handed the papers to him. He pretended to be interested in what he was reading, even though he was the one who had dictated the offer to Steve. "Wow, that's pretty generous, don't you think?"

"Exceptionally generous, and so was the first offer. But I know my grandmother won't sell."

That conversation had happened right before he left for the bank with the deposit. Now, as he glanced up at the mirror before changing lanes, Eliot was slightly startled to see his uncle's face looking back. He jumped a bit then looked again, only to realize it was a trick of the lights…or his mind, he wasn't sure which.

All he knew with absolute certainty was that he did not want to see this face when he looked in a mirror. He was not his uncle, nor did he want to become his uncle. His uncle would have taken that recipe book when Sophie offered it weeks ago. His uncle would *lose* the bank deposit and throw the small store into financial turmoil. He was not his uncle. And because he was not his uncle, he would find a compromise that did not involve destroying these people.

The next morning, Eliot was filling the front counters and Mae was filling the cash drawer when he decided to broach the subject.

"Mama Mae, you ever think about what you will do when you retire?"

"Retire? Me?"

He smiled. She sounded like the idea was so far off in the future, it was too soon to consider. "Yes, you. If anyone's earned the right to retire it would be you. Maybe go find yourself a young boyfriend."

She chuckled, shaking a finger at him. "You're a charmer, El. That's what you are."

He winked at her. "But seriously, you ever think about it? I'm sure if you tried, you could probably get a good price for this place."

She suddenly looked indignant. "I can't sell this place! My husband built this place with his own hands." She shook her head, and her sweeping became more erratic. "No, I can't sell this place. This is the legacy to Sophie, and any of our grandchildren who want to take an interest."

Eliot sat the now-empty tray on top of the counter. "What if the offer was enough to take care of all your grandchildren?"

She laughed. "Who would offer that much for this place?"

He shrugged. "You never know."

After lunch, he went out to his car for privacy and made a call to Steve asking him to rewrite the offer.

The next day when the new offer arrived via courier, Eliot expected a different response, but Sophie's reaction was much the same. And no matter how hard he tried he could not get her to show the offer to her grandmother. It all came down to unnecessarily upsetting her grandmother. Eliot didn't think Mae was nearly as fragile as her granddaughter thought she was.

So he happened to mention the two new offers to Mae when he saw her alone. But Sophie was right—Mae wasn't the slightest bit interested, even though the offer would mean a generous legacy for her grandchildren.

The clock was ticking, and Eliot could not seem to find a way to break through their shells of resistance. And he wasn't sure how many more trusting smiles from this pair of women he could stand. He knew he was coming to care more and more about Sophie and her grandmother, and the idea of leaving them devastated was not an option he was willing to accept.

He had to find a way to get them to sell and prove to his uncle that he was strong enough to take over the company at the same time. Then there was the whole *I want you, I don't want you* vibe he was getting from Sophie.

One minute, she was stroking his arms and telling him how much she appreciated his help, and the next she was practically ignoring him. One minute she was rubbing against him, giving him a hard-on that felt like a steel rod in his pants, and the next she was looking at him as if he were an alien just landed from another planet. Most days he didn't know if he was coming or going.

The combined pressure of living two lives was becoming too much, and what had started out as just a bad idea was rapidly becoming one of the most disastrous decisions of his life. He hoped he could find a way out of it before it was too late.

Chapter 11

Eliot paced the floor of his condo that evening. He couldn't go on like this. Despite what Uncle Carl said, these were good people. They were not the enemy. He stopped in front of the window and looked out over the city. How could something as soft and sweet as Sophie Mayfield ever be his enemy?

But what choice did that leave him? He'd spent his whole life working to take over Fulton Foods. All the long days and nights working in the kitchen, even as a teen, learning everything he could. He'd even designed his degree program around what he thought he would need. A combination of business and marketing. Instead of going away on spring break like his friends, he'd always returned to Memphis, spending not only breaks but summer vacations on the floor of the plant. He was so close to taking over the reins of the company. He'd made connections at all levels of the business, and all he had to do was put this competitor out of business. It wasn't anything he hadn't done before.

He started pacing again. The problem was he'd never gotten this close before. He'd never taken the time to meet the people involved before, to see the effects of his machinations. He'd never fallen for a woman like Sophie before.

How was he suppose to continue to go in there every day for however long and look them in the face, knowing what he was planning? On some level, it would be easier to simply take the book and be done with it. That would satisfy his uncle, and eventually the little bakery would recover.

He stopped suddenly. That *would* solve everything, wouldn't it? Just take the book. Then he'd never have to see Sophie again, and eventually he'd be able to forget her. Wouldn't he? It would crush Mama Mae, but so would watching her bakery be taken apart brick by brick.

Before he could talk himself out of it, Eliot grabbed his keys and headed out of the condo. Forty-five minutes later he was pulling up in front of the quiet bakery. It was dark, but Eliot knew Sophie was in the back.

He sat for a moment, thinking and planning, working out the details in his head. The office and her sleeping quarters were both in the back part of the store. But the office was on one end and the small apartment was on the other. This time of night, if she were still awake, she would probably be watching TV.

If he came in the back door and stayed close to the wall, she would never hear him. He could get into the office and slip right back out with the book. Then disappear into the night, never to be seen or heard from again.

Turning off his car, he glanced around. The little sleepy town was completely dark. Eliot was pretty sure even the police went home at night, since he'd never seen a patrol car on the streets after dark. If he hadn't spent the last few weeks working here, he would have never believed towns like this still existed.

He crept around to the back of the building. Using the set of keys she'd given him, he carefully, quietly, opened the back door. Eliot stepped inside and gently closed the door behind him. The kitchen was pitch-black and it took a moment for his eyes to adjust. As he moved farther inside, he could see a light coming from Sophie's apartment. He silently cursed. She was still awake.

He headed in the direction of the office, creeping along the wall, careful not to bump into anything, moving with the stealth of a cat burglar. Then he was standing in the office doorway.

The desk was cluttered with papers and files. Sophie kept a messy desk but was surprisingly organized despite it. On a corner of the desk, where it sat most of the time, was the large book. He swallowed hard, crossed the room and picked it up.

He stood frowning at the book for several seconds, convincing himself that the tingling in his fingers was completely imaginary. All he had to do now was walk back out the door with it. Just turn around, walk out the back door, get in his car and drive away. That was all he had to do. Just leave…. Just leave.

Five minutes later, he still stood in the exact same spot, holding the book. He released a deep sigh. "What the hell am I doing?" he muttered to himself, before putting the book back. As he turned to leave, he realized the whole evening had been a waste of time. He could have no more taken her book tonight than he could have the day Sophie offered it to him.

Careful to keep quiet, he moved out of the office and stayed against the wall as he worked his way back to the door. He was almost there when he heard a voice that froze his blood in his veins.

"El."

The whispered word came to him from Sophie's apartment. He looked in the direction, expecting to see her sitting in her doorway, watching him in the dark. But instead all he saw was just the faint light from the room.

"El."

He frowned, wondering if it were his imagination. Was she actually calling his name? Or saying something that just sounded amazingly similar?

"El." His eyes widened. Definitely his name.

He stood torn, knowing he should just go out the door and drive away as quickly as possible, but he couldn't. Not until he checked on her. What if she was hurt—in fact, she *did* kind of sound like she was in pain.

He moved along the wall, still careful. He glanced around, fairly certain he was alone in the kitchen, but he double-checked anyway. As he came to her apartment, he was in no way prepared for what he saw.

Eliot was certain he'd never seen anything so incredibly beautiful in his life.

She was spread wide open on the small twin bed, her beautiful, dark brown body completely exposed. Her soft blue cotton gown lay unbuttoned beneath her, her head against the pillow, eyes closed. The small fingers of one hand manipulated the tiny piece of flesh at her opening and the other toyed with one hardened nipple. It was the fulfillment of his most recent wet dream being acted out before his eyes. And best of all, it was his name on her lips, as she reached for the final destination.

There was so much to explore, so much to see. He'd wanted to see this view of her from the moment he'd met her, and she was more than he even imagined. Long, slender, flawless brown legs lay apart, slightly bent at the knees, revealing a dark pink opening covered by a thatch of raven-black curls. Even the unattractive white cast on her leg could not hinder the arousing picture. Her small torso was just as perfectly formed. Small, proud breasts, just enough for a large handful, with dark aroused nipples pointing to the sky, led down to a tiny waist and rounded hips.

Hips that bucked even as he watched. "Oh, El, yes! Oh yes!" Completely oblivious to his presence, she busily worked her fingers to bring herself to climax. And at some point, Eliot had stopped breathing as he watched the erotic show before him.

How many times had she masturbated and used his image as inspiration? How ever many times had been a waste! He would have been more than eager to provide her with the real thing.

"Oh, yes! Oh, El, yes!" she cried out, as her back arched and her hips lifted off the bed.

His eyes widened in amazement. From his angle he could literally see the wetness released by her body drenching her fingers. Eliot had had his fair share of lovers, but this was the first time he'd ever had this kind of ringside seat. He'd had no idea what he'd been missing out on.

Feeling slightly annoyed and a touch angry, he quietly crossed the room to stand over the bed, and waited.

Soon she floated down from her orgasm, released a great sigh of relief and opened her eyes…then wider, as if slightly confused by what she was seeing. Then he knew reality had caught up with her because she gasped in horror and scrambled to cover her body.

"Oh, my God! What are you doing here?!" she cried, pulling at the sheet at the end of the bed. Eliot grabbed the other end of the sheet and pulled back. "Stop, El! What are you doing here?!"

"At the moment, wishing I would've arrived a few minutes sooner."

Her large brown eyes widened even more, and she looked like she was going to burst into tears. "You saw?!"

"Every perfect inch of you."

"You saw what I— Oh, this can't be happening. This *can't* be happening!" She tried to bury her head in the covers, but Eliot was still holding on to the other end. "Stop it!" She tugged harder.

"Then come out and look at me."

He watched her shoulders slump beneath the covers. "Haven't you seen enough already?"

"Not nearly." He tried to hide his smile. "Why didn't you say anything?"

"What exactly was I suppose to say, El?" She peeked her head out, her brown eyes looked so open and vulnerable. "'Oh, by the way, El, when you get finished buttering those tarts, could you drop by my bedroom and *do me?*'" she said in an overly bright voice.

He grinned. "And I would've said the tarts can wait."

Apparently, that was the wrong answer, because she stuck her head back under the covers. Eliot sat down on the bed beside her, trying to ignore his growing erection. Try as he might, and despite her humiliation, his mind could not let go of what he'd just witnessed.

"Sophie." He reached and gently peeled the covers from her hand. Then, realizing he was holding the hand she'd masturbated with, he brought it to his lips and licked her fingers.

She snatched her hand back. "Don't."

"Why not?" he huffed. "You cut me out of all the good stuff. Can't I at least have the leftovers?"

She looked at him for a moment, then pulled her knees up to her chest and scooted up on the bed away from him. "Uh no, I can see where this is going, and...no."

Eliot tilted his head to the side watching her in confusion. "No?"

"You heard me."

The annoyed, angry feeling returned full force. "You'd rather do it yourself?"

"I don't have a choice!" she snapped, then instant mortification came over her face. "Can this night get any worse?"

"What do you mean you don't have a choice? I'm sitting right here—on your bed. Ready, willing and sure-as-hell able."

"El...I never meant for you to see what you did. But there is a lot of difference between masturbating while thinking of a man I find attractive and actually getting involved with that man in a real relationship."

"Yes, there is. And from what I see, a relationship would be nothing but an improvement on what you're doing."

"What if it doesn't work out?"

"What? The relationship?"

She nodded.

"I don't understand the question."

"Yes you do. Things don't work out between us, maybe it even deteriorates to the point where we no longer like each other. Then I'm out of a much-needed baker, and you're out of a job."

"And you call *me* cynical."

"I like you—and I don't mean that I just find you sexually inviting. I mean I really like you." She smiled. "I like talking to you, I like flirting with you and I don't want to mess that up."

"We won't." He shifted his body toward her, placing a hand on either side of her body. "Let me tell you what is going to happen." His eyes roamed over her form. "I'm going to stand up and undress and crawl into this bed with you and make love to you like nothing your imagination could conjure.

"Then tomorrow, I will come in here and do my job like the professional I am, and you will manage this store like the professional you are. And then tomorrow night when everyone has left for the day, I will come back in here and once again take you in my arms and you will welcome me into your body and we will make love until we're both exhausted. And we will continue like that until either we no longer want the lovemaking or we want more from each other."

"You make it sound so easy, but I've never been a big fan of casual sex."

"Sweetheart, there is nothing casual about what I want from you. *I want you to want more,* and I plan to make that my single most important objective."

She shook her head doubtfully. "I don't know, El. I can see all the things that could go wrong with that plan."

"Can you see the things that could go right?"

She looked up into his eyes. "Yes, but they feel more like dreams."

"'Nothing happens unless first a dream.'"

"Did you just steal that from someone?"

He grinned. "Carl Sandburg."

She frowned. "Are you sure you're a baker?"

El forced himself to keep his grin in place, despite the fact that her question was more than a little unsettling. "You've tasted my pastries. What do you think?"

She smiled. "That you are extremely talented in the kitchen." After a moment, she pulled back the covers revealing her body to him. "Let's see what you can do in the bedroom."

El looked at this beautiful woman, and wondered how he had stumbled into this dream come true. Suddenly, he reached forward and pulled back the sheet as far as he could. Then he reached over her and spread the nightgown beneath her, just as it had been when he'd entered the room.

Then gently, and careful of her injured leg, he parted her thighs, propping up her legs.

"Perfect," he cooed, standing to look at his handiwork. "You're beautiful."

Quickly he unbuttoned his own shirt, taking it off and tossing it aside.

"How long?" As his shoes came off, and then his pants, he watched her expression change.

"What?" she whispered.

"How long have you been doing this? Denying us both?"

She turned her head to the side, suddenly embarrassed by her naked lust. Eliot moved quickly, turning her face back to his, and his lips covered hers. "I want to know." He'd broken the kiss to look down at her, as he gently fitted his body to hers. "How many nights could I have been here with you like this? Holding you in my arms, instead of lying alone in a cold bed?" Before she could answer, his mouth came back over hers, prying her lips apart and forcing his way inside. Her arms came up and wrapped around his neck.

He pulled away from her, fumbled in his jeans for his wallet and came out with a single condom. Quickly he donned the latex covering, and then he was in her arms again. Positioning himself against her opening, he held himself perfectly still. "Say it."

"What?" She breathed against his neck, needing him to finish what he'd started in the worst way.

"I want to hear you say my name, the way you did before."

She pulled at his hips, moaning in frustration. "Please…" Her head turned left and right on the pillow, as she fought back the rising tide.

Gently he pushed inside, fitting just the wide mushroom head inside her. "Does that help?" he whispered in her ear. She instantly came apart, bucking and bucking and pulling him inside her until he was touching her core.

"Yes! Oh, El, yes!" She clung to his shoulders, her sharp little nails digging into his skin. As Eliot felt his own release charging to the tip of his penis, he was still not sure whether he was really holding this woman or if in fact this was a dream.

Chapter 12

A week later, as she scooted through the store in her chair, Sophie felt as if she were floating along on cloud nine. The past week had been everything El promised.

He was still doing his job to perfection, she was working unhindered by the relationship, and no one had a clue as to what went on in the back room at night. And, oh…what was happening in the back room at night!

True to his word, the man had skills. Her body still tingled with remembered sensations. The way he touched her; those big, strong hands moved over every inch of her body with confidence. There was something in his touch that was not a question, but a demand.

She'd had lovers, and the one thing they'd all had in common was what she called *the asking touch*. The way they'd touch her as if almost afraid to, waiting to be rejected or be given the go-ahead to do more. El didn't ask, and he sure as hell didn't wait for approval. *He took,* and the sensation was thrilling. But at the same time, he was incredibly gentle, always careful of her leg.

She rolled to the front of the store, a box of juices on her lap. As she rolled by the front window, El was outside cleaning the windows, a bottle of Windex glass cleaner in one hand and a paper towel in the other. He saw her through the glass and winked. She grinned back, giddy as a schoolgirl. She rolled over to the refrigerated dairy case and began refilling it.

Just one more thing to love about El, she thought. His willingness to chip in wherever there was work to be done. Even so, her grandmother had qualms about putting their expensive baker to work cleaning windows, sweeping floors or anything else.

While she was loading the dairy case, Mae had gone back to the kitchen. Feeling mischievous, Sophie unbuttoned the top two buttons of her blouse before turning to roll back by the window, and she got the instant reaction she wanted. El's eyes immediately went to her open top. He dropped the bottle of glass cleaner and quickly came inside.

Without hesitation, he reached inside her top, slipping his hand inside her bra to cup one breast. He bent and took her mouth, prying her lips open. His tongue pushed inside and she opened her face to his, eager for more. He knelt beside her, continuing to devour her mouth, even as his fingers went to work on the rest of her buttons.

"El!" She quickly covered his hands with her own, as it suddenly hit her. She was sitting right in front of newly cleaned glass windows, with her lover's hand in her top and her whole staff just a few feet away in the kitchen. "We can't."

He sat back on his heels, looking at her with a playful expression. Suddenly, his head swooped down, digging into her top.

"El!" She pushed at his head.

He kissed the top of her exposed breast, then he ran his lips up her neck to her lips.

"Someone could walk by the window! Or Grandma could walk back in!"

He looked up at her with an expression of pure mischief on his face, his amber eyes twinkling. "That will teach you not to taunt me."

"Oh, I can't stand you!" She laughed before turning to roll away.

Remembering her top, she stopped and buttoned it up. She glanced over her shoulder to see El standing by the door watching her.

"Tease," he said, but there was a soft smile on his lips.

She only winked in response before rolling on into the kitchen.

Later that night, the staff had gone for the day and the store had been closed up for the night, Sophie lay in Eliot's arms on the tiny bed.

"I know my father thought I was doing it to be contrary, but at the time it seemed important that a Mayfield inherited the Mayfield Bakery."

"Did you legally change your name?"

"Yes."

"And none of your family wanted to help?"

"It's kind of hard to believe, but my grandparents had five children, and out of all of them not a single one was interested in keeping the bakery open."

He kissed her forehead. "I'm sorry, sweetheart."

She glanced up at him, slightly confused. "Sorry for what?"

"Sorry that this responsibility fell to you, although I understand why you did it."

She smiled. "I know you do." She shifted her body until she was over him.

"Watch your leg," he said, helping her get comfortable. He wrapped his arm under her uninjured leg, bending it up a little more.

"Hmmm, that's nice." He felt her moist opening against the head of his penis.

She sighed, sinking down on his stiff rod. "I love the way you feel inside me. It's so…right." Bracing herself against his shoulders, she lifted her body and slid down on him again. "So good," she moaned.

Sophie rocked against him, feeling him in the deepest part of her being, and knowing if she could she would keep him there forever. She took what he offered and tried hard not to think about what was happening in her heart. Because she knew she was falling in love with El.

He was everything she had ever imagined she could want in

a husband. He was warm, and funny, sexy and thoughtful. He adored her grandmother almost as much as she did, and even his occupation fit perfectly into her life.

More and more she found herself daydreaming about the life they could have together. And he was right: they were able to have their affair and develop their relationship without it interfering with the store.

Feeling his throbbing organ pulsing inside her, Sophie clinched against him and pushed down harder, feeling the pressure building in her core. She was close, so close. Sophie looked down at El, and watched with joy as an expression of pure, agonizing bliss covered his handsome face. His eyes were closed and he was just reveling in the pleasure. Pleasure she was giving him. The thought of him being this way with another woman tore at her insides. The thought of him leaving one day was unimaginable. They'd been lovers for only a week, and she was already terrified of losing him.

Sitting back as much as possible, Sophie pushed harder against him wanting to take him with her, she was so close….

He reached up and grabbed her small breast, which seemed to fit perfectly in his palm. He pounded into her body, as his breathing became shorter and shorter.

Sophie knew she was about to come, and she bit down on her lip hard to hold back the words that were eager to escape. She'd had to do this several times in the past few days. Holding her eyes tightly closed as the orgasm washed over her, she confessed in her heart what she could not with her lips. *I love you, El! I love you with all my heart! Please don't leave me!*

The next day was the Fourth of July, and the temperature was well up in the nineties, and even though they propped the back door open the kitchen was still scorching hot. Being a holiday, there were no large orders to get out, and things had slowed down after lunch, so El, Sophie, Dante and Lonnie had decided to walk down the street to the Icy Palace Ice Cream stand.

Lonnie and Dante walked about a half block ahead of Eliot, who was pushing Sophie's chair. "Do they seem too close to you?"

Sophie asked, watching as the young couple playfully bumped against each other.

"What do you mean?"

"You know…close, like *we're* close." She glanced up at him and was surprised to find him looking directly down at her. "What are you doing?"

"Looking down your blouse, of course. What do you think I'm doing?"

She laughed, and then, realizing he was serious, laughed louder. "You have no shame."

His eyebrows crinkled. "Why do you think I volunteered for this outing? Because I was dying for soft serve?" He shook his head. "No, there's my tasty treat." He grinned. "And it's just as lickable and delicious as ice cream."

She shook her head and returned her eyes to the teenagers. "You didn't answer my other question."

"What do you want to know? Do I think Dante and Lonnie are sleeping together? Yes, I do. In fact, I'm pretty damn sure they are."

She looked at him, stunned. "Really? What makes you so certain?"

Eliot hesitated thoughtfully. "Your little cousin likes to flirt with me when no one's around."

"What?!"

"Seriously. And the last time she did, I thought I was going to have to take on that young buck. The look in his eyes left little doubt."

"About what?"

"About his wanting to whoop my ass, that's what."

She stared up at him for a moment, then shook her head doubtfully. "No, you must've misunderstood her."

His mouth twisted sarcastically. "Okay."

"Really—Lonnie wouldn't do that."

"Okay."

"Stop saying that!"

"O—" His mouth snapped shut. They continued on in silence until they had almost reached the ice cream stand. Finally, Eliot said, "I can prove it."

"How?"

"Watch." He rolled her chair up to the window, where Dante and Lonnie were already placing their orders. Sophie watched as he discreetly wedged his way between the couple, and to her amazement Lonnie's attention turned completely to Eliot.

Just as he said, Dante watched him with daggers in his eyes as Eliot playfully joked with Lonnie, and placed his order. As he turned to walk away, she listened as Lonnie changed her order to what he had requested.

"Well?" He pushed her chair to a group of benches and sat down beside her.

"Well, what?"

"Did you see Dante's reaction?"

"Yes." She bit her bottom lip thoughtfully. "That was a bit concerning. I may sit him down and explain about Lonnie to him."

El's eyes narrowed on her face. "Sophie, don't make the mistake of putting this all on Dante. You may be surprised to learn he knows more about Lonnie than you do. I know you're protective of your cousin because of her developmental problems, but you may need to take a closer look. Regardless of whatever problems she may have, she's a nineteen-year-old girl."

"I appreciate your take on it, El. I do. But you don't know what you're talking about."

El looked directly into her eyes for several seconds. "Things are not always what they seem, Sophie."

"I know that."

"No, I don't think you do. You seem to have this black-white philosophy, but the world is more complicated than that."

"I don't want to talk about this anymore."

"That's fine. Just remember what I said. Sometimes things are not what they seem."

That night El made love like a man possessed. He gave her no rest. Repeatedly taking her to the edge of ecstasy, only to pull her back. His mouth was everywhere. It was as if he were trying to devour every inch of her. Her breasts, her stomach. Pulling her legs apart, he buried his mouth inside her and she came apart in his arms.

Then he was rising up over her, guiding his hard erection into her body and pumping into her with wild energy. His strong arms were braced on either side of her head, and she was helpless to do anything but experience orgasm after orgasm. When she finally fell asleep it was well after three in the morning. When her alarm clock went off at five, El was gone.

She leaned up on her elbows, looking around the empty, tiny room. Something happened last night. Something she still did not understand. There was still so much about him she did not know. So much that did not make any sense.

El did not show up at his regular start time, but Sophie refused to call him at the risk of sounding like an obsessed lunatic. As soon as Dante arrived a little after eight, Sophie called him into the office.

"Can you close the door?" She scooted her chair to allow closing the door of the small office.

He leaned against the door. "What's up, Sophie?"

Dante was tall and lanky, and even at nineteen it was obvious to see he still had some growing to do. From what Sophie knew he'd barely finished high school and had no real ambitions toward college. He was happy with his job at the bakery and living in his parent's garage.

Sophie had given him the job because in the first interview she'd sensed in him the kind heart he later showed himself to have. He'd also proved himself to be honest and loyal. But for all that, she could not simply look the other way or condone what he was doing with her cousin.

"I walked to talk to you about your relationship with Lonnie." He visibly stiffened. "Oh?"

"Dante, I know—or, at least, I think I know what's going on between you two."

She watched his eyes dart around as if he were going to deny it, then he seemed to come to some kind of a decision, because he looked right at her and said, "We love each other."

Sophie felt her stomach drop. There it was. Confirmation.

"Are you sleeping with Lonnie?"

He looked down at his feet. "No disrespect, but I don't see how that's any of your business."

"Dante, I believe you *think* you're in love, but Lonnie is not…" She tried again. "Dante, Lonnie has some problems you may not know about."

"You mean her Down syndrome?"

Sophie nodded.

"But, she's okay."

"No…she's not."

"Sophie, my little sister has Down syndrome, did you know that?"

Her eyes widened.

"I've been around people like her all my life, and if I didn't think Lonnie knew what she was doing, or understood what we were doing, I wouldn't—I couldn't." He shook his head.

Sophie felt like screaming at him to leave Lonnie alone, but she knew in her gut what the reaction would be. "She could get pregnant."

"I'm careful. We use protection. I'm going to marry her, Sophie."

"Dante, you don't understand."

"No offense, Sophie, but, maybe…you're the one who doesn't understand." He toyed with the door handle as he said, "Look, talk to Lonnie, see what she says…okay?"

Sophie swallowed the lump in her throat. "All right."

"Can I go?"

She nodded, still too shaken up and not knowing exactly how to handle this situation. It was supposed to have been a simple task of warning the boy off, not possibly confronting two people who thought themselves in love. After all, who was she to say they weren't?

Given her own shaky relationship, she was the last person to give advice on love.

Dante started to open the door, and then paused. "My sister, she has a job and her own place, and she does what she wants to do. I know there are some people with the condition who are not able to have that kind of a life, but Lonnie can. She's a lot like my sister. She's okay."

When he opened the door to leave, she caught a glimpse of El coming out of the walk-in fridge. For a brief moment, their eyes met, but neither acknowledged the other or whatever had passed between them the night before. But that night, after the store was locked up, El did not come to her.

Chapter 13

The first time Wayne bumped against him, Eliot decided it was an accident and simply ignored it. Five minutes later the other man passed him again, this time bumping a little harder. Eliot grew suspicious. The third time Wayne came shoulder to shoulder with him, Eliot stepped back and let him pass, and he could see the instant anger in the other man.

"You got something you want to say to me, Wayne?"

Wayne turned to face him, and the two men stared at each other for several moments before Wayne walked back to him, and whispered near his ear, "You have no idea how much I want to kill you right now. If this were a different place, and a different time, you would be dead already."

"What's stopping you?" Eliot asked, refusing to back down. This had been coming from the day he walked into the store.

"My love for these people," he said, and started to walk away.

"Name the where and when, I'll be there," El said, before turning back to the preparation table where he was rolling swirling buns. The attack came out of nowhere. Wayne charged at his midsection and slammed him against the walk-in freezer.

But Eliot expected the attack. He was able to shift his body with relative ease to get his arms up under the other man's body. He lifted Wayne a little, then slammed him down and was able to break free.

Wayne came at his middle again, throwing him back against the freezer once more. In the distance, Eliot could hear Lonnie screaming Sophie's name. But his attention was on breaking the choke hold Wayne had managed to get on him.

He turned, twisted, and shoved his elbow into the other man, causing him to double over.

"What is going on in here?" He heard Mae coming in from the front, but before he could tell her to get back out of the way, a wall fell on his back.

"Damn!" Dante's high-pitched squeal reflected El's true feelings. He was pinned beneath the other man, and Wayne knew it. He started punching Eliot in the sides, and each blow felt like a steel mallet pounding away at him.

There was nowhere he could go to get away from the torture, so he reached under the preparation table, grabbed a large pan and swung it upward to hit Wayne in the head.

Wayne let up long enough to cover his head, but it was all the opening Eliot needed. His sides and stomach aching, he pulled himself out from under Wayne and stumbled to his feet. He tried to catch his breath as Wayne stood, too.

One look at his face and El understood something he hadn't given much thought to before. He and Wayne were about the same age, and despite Wayne's physical advantages as a result of his weight lifting, they were both at about the same fitness level.

Wayne took that moment to swing at El. He ducked, easily escaping the blow. The two men staggered back and forth, each taking a punch now and then and occasionally landing a hit. But it didn't take long for them both to run out of steam.

Eliot, wandered out the front door needing fresh air. He sat down on the curb and realized there was blood dripping from his face. Receiving some strange stares from passersby, he started to get up and go back inside. Just then he noticed a pair of familiar men's shoes standing beside him. He looked up and up and grimaced, wondering if his face looked nearly as bad as Wayne's.

Wayne sat down on the curb next to him, and the two men just sat in silence for a long time. After what seemed an hour, Wayne finally said, "I've gotten soft working in this place."

"All those big lunches Mama Mae feeds us," Eliot said, feeling a touch bad for blaming his lack of conditioning on that sweet old lady.

Wayne huffed. "And it *is* a bakery. I'm not gonna lie and say I don't occasionally sample the goods."

The silence fell back in place for several more minutes, but Eliot had to know. "What was that about?"

"I can't stand your ass."

"I know that, but you've never come at me before today. What's changed?"

Wayne looked away down the street, and for a second Eliot didn't think he would answer. Finally, he said, "You know what's changed."

Eliot did. On some instinctual level he'd known the moment Wayne charged him. Somehow Wayne had found out about his affair with Sophie. "It's none of your business, man."

"I know." He glanced at Eliot, his hands tightening into fists, and Eliot was instantly on guard. "But I look at you and all I see is red haze. I hate you so much…for something neither one of us had any control over. Sophie thinks for herself, and she chose you. I understand that up here." He tapped his temple, and sighed heavily. "It's just going to take me a minute to accept it in here," he said and touched his chest.

Eliot couldn't help but feel sympathy for the man. It wasn't hard to imagine the pain of losing Sophie. In fact, it was becoming his worst nightmare.

The door opened behind them. "Get on in here so we can clean you up!" Mae snapped from the door. "Damn bullheaded jackas—"

The rest of the statement was cut off as the door closed. Eliot looked at Wayne with a slight smile. "You made Mama Mae curse."

"I got news for you," Wayne said. He stood and stretched out his hand to El. "She curses quite a bit when no one's around."

Eliot took the hand and allowed himself to be helped to his feet. "So? We straight?"

Wayne glanced down at the ground and nodded. "For the moment." He looked up with a small smile. "But I'm sure you'll do something else to piss me off eventually."

El sat patiently on the floor by Sophie's twin bed while she examined his bruises. She sniffed hesitantly. "Oh, yuck. Grandma used some of her stinky salve on you, didn't she?"

He scrunched his nose. "I was instructed not to wash it off for twenty-four hours."

"It stinks, but it works." She turned his head at another angle. "Wow, he really worked you over."

"Hey, I got in a couple of good punches, too."

She tilted his head up to kiss his lips, cooing, "Yes, you did, my brave warrior." Once she'd satisfied herself that he would heal, she sat back and wiped the smelly salve from her hands on a nearby towel. "So, what was that about, anyway?"

Eliot stood and started pulling his shirt over his head. "Minor disagreement."

"If that was minor, I would hate to see major."

"Did you talk to Dante?"

"Yes, and you were right. They are sleeping together. He says he wants to marry Lonnie."

"Well, there you go."

"No, not quite. Tomorrow I talk to Lonnie." She smiled up at him. "I was planning to talk to her today, but then I was distracted by your impressive display of manliness," she said.

"Ha, ha." He kicked off his boots and started on his pants. "Scoot over."

She pulled the covers to her chest, and refused to budge. "Not until you tell me one thing about yourself that I do not know."

He arched an eyebrow. "What's this? The price of admission?"

Her healthy leg shot out of the covers and kicked, catching his upper back thigh.

"Ouch."

"Let's try this again—without the insults."

"What kind of woman are you?!" He rubbed at his bottom. "I get my butt kicked all over by one of your little henchmen, come in here looking for a little sympathy, and what do you do? Kick my butt!"

"Sorry, but I'm serious about this, and you're making jokes. You're so secretive, yet you want me to believe you want a committed relationship. Prove it. Tell me at least one thing I do not know."

He sighed. "One thing you don't know…hmm."

"It could be anything. Something about your career, your family, your childhood. Anything! I'm not picky."

"I'm an only child."

"Really?"

"Yes, now scoot," he said.

She scooted over in the bed.

El climbed in beside her. "I don't like the idea of having to earn my way into your bed."

"I don't like the idea of having to earn my way into your life."

"I just have to figure out some things, that's all."

"Well, while you're working some things out, you can share at least one new thing with me every day to keep me off your back. How's that?"

With lightning speed, he flipped her over on her side and came up behind her. "How are you going to keep me off your back?" he whispered in her ear, even as his busy fingers were working their way into her moist opening.

Sophie gasped when she felt the first touch of his latex-covered penis pushing into her body. Reveling in the feel of his hands on her, she whispered back, "Who says I want to?"

Chapter 14

The next day, Eliot sat in one of the chairs in the front of the store as Mae examined his wounds and the handiwork of her homemade ointment. She nodded in satisfaction, then moved to another chair where Wayne sat, staring him down. She nodded again.

"All right, I've done all I can do for you. The rest is up to nature." Like an efficient doctor, she packed up her small box of salves and ointments and put it back behind the counter.

Wayne got up and headed back into the kitchen, but Eliot stalled a bit. He wanted to talk to Mae alone.

"Mama Mae, I just wanted to tell you how much I appreciate all your help."

She smiled. "That's what I'm here for. But I won't tolerate you and Wayne tearing this place up, you hear?" She shook her frail index finger at him. "Sophie works hard to keep this place up and running."

Eliot glanced over his shoulder. "How long has Sophie been running the store?"

"Not sure." Mae laughed. "Started when she was just a girl. Her mama and daddy didn't like her spending so much time here. Said me and Earl was putting crazy ideas in her head." Mae shrugged. "I guess they didn't like that she was more like us than them. But that wasn't our fault. It's in the blood."

"If Sophie ever wanted to sell would you be okay with that?"

"I guess I would have to be. I know I can't run this place alone anymore."

Eliot sighed in relief. Now all he had to do was talk Sophie into selling, and then she would convince her grandmother. Maybe there was a way out of this nightmare scenario after all.

"You know," Mae continued, oblivious to his plotting, "when we started this place, we always thought the kids would take over eventually."

"Why didn't they?"

"The older ones had seen too much, and the younger ones hadn't seen enough. Me and Earl, we ran into some money problems in the first part of our married years. This bakery wasn't our only effort to run a business, just the only one that lasted."

"It's not easy running a business."

"No, it's not." She picked up a rag and began wiping down the counter, and Eliot realized it was more out of habit than need. The counter was already spotless. "How did you learn to cook so good, El?"

"Culinary school," he answered automatically, but the look she gave him told him that was not the answer she was looking for. He smiled. "My mother. She was an excellent baker, and sometimes she'd let me help her. Eventually, I was coming up with my own ideas for things."

"I always said ain't nothing wrong with a mother teaching her son to cook." Mae finished the counter and slipped on a pair of plastic gloves. Then she began to arrange the pastries on the counter.

"You remind me of her," he said quietly.

"Your mother?" She was consolidating the pastries on the trays in the front counter and removing the empties.

He nodded. "Look, I'll talk to you later," he said, then turned and headed back into the kitchen. He had gotten the answer he needed, now if he could just convince Sophie to go along.

He would have Steve draw up yet another offer. The new package would provide for everyone—Sophie, her grand-mother, even Dante, Lonnie and Wayne would be taken care of with a severance package. And then he could tell Sophie the truth and clear his conscience. Just the idea of it was enough to make him sigh in relief. The weight of his deceit was becoming way too heavy.

Sophie and Lonnie sat on opposite sides of the desk in her office. Lonnie was playing with the leaves of a fake plant on the corner of the desk, and Sophie was glancing through the mail, stalling for time. She had no idea how to broach the subject with Lonnie. With Dante she just said what she was thinking—but what if Lonnie got embarrassed or upset? Even though she was nineteen years old, in many ways she was much younger.

"Lonnie?"

"Hmm?" She looked up at Sophie with liquid-chocolate eyes, much like her own.

"You and Dante…do you like him?"

She nodded, continuing to toy with the plant.

"Like a girl likes a boy like him? Or like a friend?"

She frowned thoughtfully. "Both."

Sophie cleared her throat, deciding to just go for it. "Lonnie, do you understand what sex is?"

Lonnie laughed. "Of course, Sophie. Don't be silly."

"Are you having sex with Dante?"

Lonnie stopped playing with the plant, her eyes coming up to meet Sophie's. "Who told you that?"

Seeing she was becoming alarmed, she reached across the desk and took her hand. "No one, no one said anything. But I can tell something is happening between you two. Are you?"

Lonnie looked her directly in the eyes with a clarity Sophie had rarely seen. "I love Dante and he loves me, and we are going to be married," she said.

Sophie's eyes narrowed on her face. "Did Dante tell you he would marry you if you had sex with him?"

She shook her head. "No—afterwards." She quickly covered her mouth as if she had said too much.

Sophie swallowed. Things were coming into perspective, but she still felt as if she were treading on thin ice. "Lonnie, what makes you think you love Dante? Because you had sex with him?"

She continued to toy with the plant for a long time before finally answering: "He doesn't treat me like I'm stupid."

Sophie frowned. "No one treats you like you're stupid."

"You do." She nodded. "Sometimes."

Sophie wanted to shake her head and deny it, but obviously it was how Lonnie felt. "When have I ever treated you like you were stupid?"

"All the time," Lonnie said. She glanced up and quickly looked away. "I know you don't mean it bad, but sometimes you act like I can't do anything. All you let me do around here is sweep and carry boxes."

Sophie watched her thoughtfully. "I didn't realize you wanted to do more."

She smiled shyly. "Sometimes when we leave on deliveries, Dante takes me by the old abandoned mill, and then he lets me get behind the wheel and drive around the lot." She toyed with a leaf. "I'm getting good at it, too. He said after we get married, he was going to let me take driving lessons."

Sophie was listening attentively now, seeing a side of her little cousin she'd never known existed. "What else does Dante let you do?"

She glanced at Sophie again. "He lets me talk to customers, but…"

"But?"

"But, sometimes, he won't let me talk to the men. He said some of them only pretend to be friendly, but they're just trying to—you know."

Sophie swallowed. "Yes, I know." She waited a moment, wondering if she should speak her thought, then said, "But, you don't think Dante is being nice just to…you know?"

She shook her head. "Oh, no. I swear I had the hardest time getting ~~him to~~ do it. He kept saying no, over and over and over," she said, and she shook her head in exasperation.

Sophie's eyes widened again. "It was *your* idea?"

Lonnie retreated into the shy shell, her shoulders hunched in and she looked back to the fake plant. Sophie realized she may have said more than she intended. "It's okay, Lonnie, if you did. I was just wondering."

Slowly, she nodded.

Sophie sat back with a heavy sigh, thinking how things could change so drastically in just a few moments. How had she not seen all this happening around her? She started thinking back to when and how Dante and Lonnie had started spending so much time together. And it hit her in a flash: the friendship or relationship had been initiated when Lonnie started tagging along after Dante, and the boy had begrudgingly taken her along.

"Lonnie, can I ask how long you and Dante have been... having sex?"

She frowned thoughtfully again, then shrugged. "I don't know—a while."

"Before Christmas?"

She shook her head no. "No, around Valentine's Day, because Mama Mae was making all those pink heart-shaped cookies. Those were so good."

Sophie smiled. "Yes they were."

"El cooks good, too." Lonnie smiled, but there was something about the smile that sent a signal to Sophie. "He's cute, too. I like his hair."

"Lonnie, El's not like Dante."

Lonnie sighed. "I know. Dante already said if I had sex with anyone else he wouldn't marry me."

Sophie frowned, wondering how often Dante issued warnings like that. "When did Dante tell you that?"

"Once when I met this cute boy by the playground, where we go sometimes after deliveries. Dante made the boy leave, but he was nice. Then there was that time the customer was saying hello, Dante told me not to smile so much at the customers. And then I was talking to El, and he got mad about that, too."

"Lonnie, you can't go around having sex with anyone and everyone. You understand? Something could happen, you could get pregnant, or…worse."

She shook her head. "No, Mama Mae took me to the doctor and now I take a pill every morning so I won't get a baby, until me and Dante want to."

"Grandma took you to the doctor?!" Seeing Lonnie's alarmed expression, she tried to reign in her outrage. It was just too shocking to realize, apparently everyone knew about Dante and Lonnie except her. Even her seventy-year-old grandmother had known. "When did Grandma take you to the doctor?"

Lonnie was watching her with fearful eyes now. "I'm sorry, Sophie. I didn't mean to do anything wrong. I shouldn't take the pills?"

Sophie swallowed hard and forced a smile. "No, Lonnie, no—take the pills. The pills are a good thing." She tilted her head to the side. "I'm just a little surprised Grandma didn't tell me, that's all. Okay?"

Lonnie nodded warily.

"Okay. You can go back to work now. And Lonnie, thank you for talking to me."

She smiled. "It was fun. I like talking to you Sophie."

As Lonnie turned to leave, Sophie called out. "And—I *am* going to give you more things to do around here. Would you like that?"

Her smile brightened. "Yes. Can I learn how to cook?"

Sophie smiled back. "You can do anything you want to do." And as Sophie watched her cousin leave the room, for the first time she realized it was true.

"At what point were you going to tell me Lonnie was having sex with Dante?"

Sophie waited for the lone customer to leave the store, and then quietly came up behind her grandmother.

Mae jumped in startled surprise. "Oh, Lord, Sophie! You trying to give me a heart attack?"

"Lonnie, Grandma. Why didn't you tell me about Lonnie?"

"Didn't see any need to."

"You didn't think I should know that my deliveryman and my mentally challenged cousin were lovers?" she whispered.

Mae shook her head. "No, I didn't. In case you've forgotten, I am Lonnie's legal guardian, not you. Not that it matters, considering both of them are over the age of consent."

Another customer entered the store, and Sophie waited patiently for her grandmother to take care of him. Her brain was busy processing all she'd learned. And it bothered her a little that El, who'd only been working there a short while, had already figured all this out.

Once the customer left, she picked up where they'd left off. "Well?"

Mae glanced at her over her shoulder. "Well, what?"

"Lonnie. You took her to get birth-control pills and didn't even tell me."

As if she'd reached her end, Mae turned fully to her granddaughter, and Sophie knew the winds had changed when she put both hands on her hips. "Let's get something straight, Sophie. I know you think I'm some senile old woman, but don't forget I managed to raise five children, three of which were girls, long before you came into the world. And although I appreciate your help, I was also running this store long before you came into the world. I did what I thought was best for Lonnie and I don't owe you, her trifling mama or anyone else an explanation for the decisions I made regarding that child. Is that understood?"

Sophie nodded dumbly.

Mae shook her head. "Sometimes, girl, you take too much on your shoulders. You're not responsible for the whole world. Certainly not Lonnie and me." Mae walked back into the kitchen, leaving Sophie alone in the front of the store.

"But sometimes, I feel like it," Sophie said, then followed her grandmother into the kitchen.

Chapter 15

It had become crystal clear to Eliot that subtle was not going to work on the Mayfield women. So, he'd decided to try a different tack. What he called *Operation Sell! Sell! Sell!*

As he swept the front walk entryway of the store a week later, he watched as it was implemented. A real estate agent named Gill Childers pulled up in front of the store. Completely ignoring Eliot as he'd been paid to do, he entered the store and walked up to the counter.

"Hello, ma'am. Are you the owner?"

Mae nodded, watching the man suspiciously.

Eliot smiled to himself. He would trust Mae's instincts any day.

"My name is Gill—Gill Childers—and I would like to talk to you about your store. I have an offer that would knock your socks off! Would you like to hear it?"

"Well, my granddaughter runs the bus—"

"Say no more! Can I speak to this granddaughter? My client had authorized me to make this offer, but it is for a limited time only."

"Sophie!" Mae called to the back, but Lonnie showed up. "Lonnie, go ask Sophie to come here, please."

"Yes, ma'am." And Lonnie hurried away.

A few minutes later, Sophie rolled to the front of the store, glancing first at Eliot, then the visitor. "Yes?"

"Hello, ma'am. My name is Gill—Gill Childers—and I have an offer that will knock your socks off. My client has authorized me to offer you…" He pulled out a card and handed it to her.

Sophie's mouth dropped open. "For what?" Mae had come up behind her and Sophie handed over the card.

"Oh, good Lord," Mae breathed, reading the number on the card.

"For this store, of course!" Gill answered Sophie's question. "Now, being a strip mall, my client is assuming you don't own the building, and in that case—"

"Yes we do."

That announcement caused Eliot to look around, as well.

Gill seemed momentarily stumped. "Excuse me?"

"We were one of the first businesses here, and we were given the option to buy—we took it. We own the building."

Eliot looked away, seeing Gill fight the urge to make eye contact. This was the problem with proprietary businesses, Eliot thought. Certain facts regarding their financial situations were hard to uncover.

"Well, that does not change the offer!" Gill rebounded. "The price on that card is for the business as it stands! You would just sign the dotted line, collect your check and walk out the front door."

"Why?" Sophie asked.

"Location, my dear. Location, Location, Location. And my client needs this particular location."

Sophie and Mae glanced at each other. "This is a ridiculous amount of money for a small bakery, Mr. Childers," Sophie finally said.

"Like I said, my client needs this particular location—and he needs it today. What do you say?"

Sophie looked shocked. "Certainly, you don't expect us to make this kind of business decision in a moment, do you?"

"Well, I need an answer immediately. This offer won't last forever. My client is in a hurry to get moving on this."

"Can I ask what he plans to do with the place? Continue to run it as a bakery? Or move everything out and create something different?"

"No offense, Ms....?"

"Mayfield."

"No offense, Ms. Mayfield, but that is a confidential matter. So when do you think I can have an answer?"

Mae bent and whispered something in Sophie's ear. Sophie nodded in agreement. "Sorry, Mr. Childers, we need to know more. That is a great sum of money, enough to provide for my whole staff, but we can't just sign over this store on a whim."

"Of course not. Of course not. Tell you what. I will give you twenty-four hours to decide. I'll be back around this time tomorrow, what do you say?"

Sophie glanced at her grandmother for confirmation. "I'd say you're wasting your time, but you are certainly welcome to come back."

"Good day, ladies." He turned and, as quickly as he had appeared, he was gone.

Eliot strolled over to Sophie's chair. "Can I see?" he asked Mae, and she handed over the card. "Wow, that's generous."

Sophie's eyes narrowed on the window. "Too generous. What is he up to?"

Mae shook her head. "Don't know, but there is something shady about that character."

Eliot wanted to scream in frustration, but held back. "Could it be that he is just doing what he said, trying to close a deal for a client who really, really wants this location?"

"For what?" Mae snapped. "One of those seedy bars where the women take off their clothes?"

Eliot shook his head. "Mama Mae, this is a strip mall, with a laundry service, dress store and video store. Who would want to put a strip club in here?"

She frowned at him. "I don't know how those men think."

"No," Sophie said thoughtfully. "He wants it for something else. Or nothing."

"What do you mean?" Eliot asked. Maybe his woman was too damn smart for her own good.

"It doesn't make any sense. Why would he want us to just leave everything and walk out the door, unless he wanted the bakery? But if that's the case, why the rush? It doesn't make any sense."

No, it didn't. Not really. But Eliot had hoped they would be so impressed by the dollar figure, realizing that it would be enough to provide for the staff, as well, that they wouldn't start asking those kinds of questions. But in the mad dash to get them out of there, Eliot had forgotten one critical thing about these two. It wasn't about money, had never been about money. For Sophie it was about proving to her family once and for all that the bakery could be more than just a financial sponge soaking up every dollar in sight. And for Mae, it was about her husband's memory and legacy. In the end, you couldn't put a price on those kinds of ambitions. And Eliot knew already that the very talented and persuasive Mr. Gill Childers would ultimately get nowhere with these two. Which meant he was back at square one.

Later that night, as they lay together in Sophie's little bed, Eliot continued to try to persuade her, but with no real energy. He'd already accepted defeat…at least for the moment.

"I was terribly shy."

"Really?"

He nodded. True to her word, Sophie had continued with her one new thing every night. And Eliot was running out of insignificant generic facts about himself. "How about you?"

"I never really thought about it, but I guess I would be considered outgoing. I have plenty of friends and was always into some school thing. But still, I always liked being here more than hanging out with my friends. So, I guess in that way I was a little different."

"Loving your grandparents is not different or odd."

"In my family, it almost is."

They lay spooned together. Eliot had placed a pillow beneath her leg for support. "So, I assume you're going to tell that real estate guy no?"

"Yes, although I doubt if anyone would ever offer us that much again."

"Then why not take the offer?" He asked the question, even though he already knew the answer.

"Because it's not about money. I mean, don't get me wrong. Money is nice. We're all in business to make money, but it's not the only thing. We have to think about our staff, as well. In a small town like Selmer, jobs are few and far between as it is. Someone like you can go anywhere and find a job, but Wayne? With his record? Or Dante, with his lack of training in anything? It's not just about me and Grandma and making a fat profit."

He kissed her shoulder. "I know. That's why I'm crazy about you."

True to his word, Gill Childers showed up the next day and accepted the rejection of his offer with grace and kindness. And Eliot could see the handwriting on the wall.

The next night, Eliot had a dream. He stood before a wall of fire and knew that somewhere behind the wall was Sophie, her grandmother and everyone at Mayfield. But someone else was there.

His uncle blocked his path, and he was holding a burning torch. Eliot knew the only way he could get to them was to get past his uncle. But as he was trying to find a way, he heard screaming. Sophie's screams as she cried out his name. There were other screams mixed in, but it was Sophie's screams that tore out his heart.

But every time he moved toward the wall, his uncle would thrust the torch at him. It soon became apparent to Eliot that he would have to risk the flames if he wanted to save Sophie. Then he heard her again, crying out his name...

"El! El, wake up! You're on my leg!"

Eliot opened his eyes to hear Sophie's very real mournful cries. He looked down and realized he'd rolled over on her cast. Quickly he shifted, moving back over. "You okay?"

She sat up, cradling the leg in her arms. "It hurts like hell!" she whimpered.

"Baby, I'm so sorry." He wrapped his arms around her and pulled her against him, not sure what else he could do. "You want to go to emergency?"

She shook her head instantly. "No, it will stop." Then suddenly, she punched his arm. "You sleep too hard! I kept calling you and calling you, and you wouldn't wake up."

"I'm sorry. I'm so sorry." He continued to hold her.

At her request, he went into the kitchen and brought back a glass of water. She took a couple of the pain pills the doctor had prescribed, and soon she was dozing in his arm again. This time, Eliot put the pillows between her legs and his, so he wouldn't repeat the incident.

He knew his dream was not connected to Sophie's aching ankle, and the disturbing images stayed with him straight through to the next morning. By the time he left her to change into clean clothes and prepare for the day, Eliot was certain he understood the symbolism of the dream. Time was running out.

Chapter 16

"After eight long weeks, finally!" Sophie glanced back at El with a cheeky grin. "Hurry up, Dr. Michelson. I have a weekend getaway waiting for me."

"Sophie, I expect you to go home and rest on this ankle, not go gallivanting around Memphis." As he spoke, the doctor's attention was fixed on the saw as he cut through the cast. "But, then again, when do you ever listen to me," he muttered.

"Don't worry, Doc, I'll take good care of her." Eliot winked at her.

Dr. Michelson finally finished sawing, then used a large forceps-type device to gently pull the two sides apart, revealing a fully healed ankle. Placing the cast to the side, the doctor ran his hand over the ankle, checking all sides. "Perfect," he finally pronounced. "Well, despite your bad behavior, the ankle still managed to heal correctly. You shouldn't have any problems with it in the future, but if you do experience any pain let me know right away, understood?"

"Yes, sir." She grinned from ear to ear, anticipating the

romantic weekend ahead of her. After the incident with Wayne, it didn't take everyone else long to figure out something was going on between them. And though, no one ever said anything directly to either of them, the feel of eyes constantly on them was becoming annoying. Both needing a break from all the unasked questions. El had promised that as soon as her cast came off, he would take her away for the weekend. So she made sure her appointment to have the cast removed was on a Friday.

Less than an hour later, they were on the freeway headed to Memphis, and Sophie was feeling as if the world could not get any better. "So, what's the plan this weekend?"

"I've developed what I call the three-*B* package."

"Three-*B*?"

He nodded, watching the road carefully all the while. "Yes, first we check into a bed-and-breakfast, a cozy little place on the river."

"Is that one *B* or two, for *bed* and *breakfast?*"

"That's one. Then we enjoy dinner and some of the best blues in the country at a club downtown."

"Hmm, sounds good so far. That's *B* number two. And three?"

"After we've enjoyed an evening of good food and great music, we come back to our cozy little bed-and-breakfast, and you…" He flashed her a quick grin. "Give up the booty."

She laughed. "You sure can kill a romantic vibe."

"What?" He frowned. "How is that not romantic?"

She shook her head. "Never mind. I can't expect you to understand. So, why does a chef from Houston know so much about Memphis?"

"What makes you think I know so much about Memphis?"

"The three-*B* package sounds like your standard get-laid combo."

"It's not." He glanced over at her. "It was created just for you."

"Really?"

"Believe it or not, before I came to work for you, I dedicated most of my time to work. I didn't date much."

"So what are you saying? Working for me inspires you to slack off?"

He chuckled. "No, but being with you does let me know that there are more important things in life than my career and ambition."

"What about the married woman?"

"Who?"

She frowned. "The woman you had the affair with, the one who got you fired."

"Oh, yeah—her. Temporary lapse in judgment."

"Well, I can overlook that lapse, because it brought you to Selmer." She leaned over and kissed his cheek. "Just don't lapse again."

"Why would I, when I have *B* number three to look forward to?"

Later than evening, they arrived at the bed-and-breakfast and were greeted by an older African-American couple, dressed in western garb, whose names were Roy and Dale. Sophie found the fact that the couple shared their names with the old Western movie and TV stars hilarious. Eliot, was not the slightest bit amused by the coincidence, but he did find her uncontrollable laughing fit funny. So in the end, they were both rolling around on the huge king-sized bed and laughing like a couple of lunatics.

They had reservations at the club for seven but made the mistake of deciding to shower together. One thing led to another, and they didn't get out of the shower until seven-twenty. Eliot called the club and, luckily, they had another opening at nine.

They were dressed and ready to go when Eliot got a call on his cell phone. He stepped out into the hall to take it, which Sophie thought was strange, but she ignored it because her ankle was starting to hurt.

She attempted to stand on it, and began limping around the room hoping to build the strength in it. "Ouch!" She clutched the end of the bed, just as El was reentering the room.

"What's wrong?" he rushed to her, and braced her against his side.

She forced a smile through the pain. "Nothing."

El frowned down at her leg. "Is your ankle hurting?"

She shook her head. "No, not at all, let's get ready to go."

He stared at her for several long moments, and she fought to keep the pained expression off her face.

"Liar." Suddenly, he reached behind her knees and swooped her up in his arms, carrying her to the side of the bed.

"El, we're going to miss our reservation."

"So be it. We're not going anywhere with you in pain." He gently placed her against the pillows at the head of the bed. And although she would never admit it, it felt good to be off her foot.

"El! I didn't come all this way to sit in a hotel room!" She pounded her fist against the comforter, feeling childish as she did it, but the frustration was real. This was suppose to be their special weekend, and her stupid ankle was about to ruin it.

El went into the bathroom and came back with a warm, damp cloth and wrapped it around her ankle.

"Tell you what," she ran her hand over his soft locks, "how about a compromise?"

He turned his head and looked at her. "This should be good. Let's hear it."

"Take me to the club tonight, and we can stay in the rest of the weekend."

"And how do you propose to get to the club when you can't stand?"

"I can stand." She moved to get off the bed.

"No!"

Sophie stopped suddenly and her eyes widened at the harsh tone, and El quickly shook his head.

"Sorry, baby. I can't stand to see you in pain." He sat down beside her with a heavy sigh. "Tell you what, since it's obvious you're not going to give me any peace if we don't go tonight. We'll go, but I'm carrying you. Deal?"

She smiled widely. "Deal."

He insisted on carrying her to the car, but Sophie didn't mind. There were few places in the world she enjoyed more than being snuggled against his chest. And Dale and Roy thought the whole display was extremely romantic.

They had a slight disagreement when they arrived at the club after Sophie realized Eliot intended to carry her inside the club.

They compromised by having one of the club's guest wheelchairs brought out to her.

Sophie was a little disappointed with the turn of the evening, because she'd been waiting over two months to dance with El, but he promised her they would have other chances, and she wanted to believe him.

The club was everything he told her it would be, with good food and great music. She'd never heard of the band and didn't know why, considering how talented they were. The band played blues and their versions of many popular R & B songs.

A photographer came by and took their picture. El bought two copies, one for each of them. They shared a barbeque rib platter with all the trimmings. And by the time they left late that night, the band was starting to pack up their equipment.

When they got back to the bed-and-breakfast, Dale was the only one awake, and she was just waiting for them so that she could lock the door for the night. By the time El crawled into bed next to her, Sophie was certain she'd had the best day of her life.

"Trust me," El was whispering in her ear, even as he tied her hands together with the silk scarf he'd pulled out of his overnight bag. He glanced down at her bare legs, then shook his head. "I really had my heart set on tying your feet, as well, but not with your ankle still bothering you," he said.

Sophie lay naked beneath his straddling form, finding herself disturbingly aroused by the sense of helplessness the ties brought on. "Been thinking about this a lot, have you?"

"You have no idea," he muttered, as he reached for another scarf to cover her eyes.

She shook her head. "No, El."

He looked directly into her eyes. "Trust me, gorgeous. I would never hurt you." He smiled. "All this will do is heighten your awareness."

She did trust him. That was not the problem. It was the fact that she was enjoying this too much that she found most troubling.

"Can I?"

She stared into his eyes for a moment before she nodded her consent. He tied the scarf behind her head, effectively blocking her sight. And he was right, because she was instantly more aware of his body over hers. The feel of his hard thighs against hers, his stiff erection laying against her stomach. Even his breathing seemed louder this way.

"You've got to trust me, gorgeous. That's the only way you can fully appreciate this," he whispered in her ear.

"I trust you," she whispered back, feeling his weight leave the bed.

She heard a rustling noise, and then a few drops of heat touched her stomach. She gasped in surprise, but the heat quickly cooled and became a comfortable warm sensation. Oil.

And then she felt his hands sliding through the liquid warmth, spreading it all over her torso, her sensitive breasts and her shoulders. Then back down over her flat stomach to the curls covering her womanhood. He spent quite a bit of time just playing in her curls, drenching them in the oil, when all she wanted was for him to continue south. To touch her where she most wanted to be touched.

She spread her legs wide in invitation, and still he ignored her most essential part, continuing to toy with her curls, his thumb brushing briefly over her hypersensitive clit. Sophie bit her lip for fear of whimpering like an animal in need.

His weight shifted again, and she could feel his body over hers, legs to legs, chest to chest, and…he rubbed against her, and she almost shot off the bed in surprise. The feel of his whole body rubbing over her oily skin was incredible.

"You like that?" he whispered. Instead of waiting for an answer his mouth swooped down on hers, demanding, taking. Prying his way between her lips, he sucked her tongue into his mouth, and Sophie felt as if she could hardly bring air into her lungs for the intense sensation.

As soon as he released her mouth, she shouted her response: "Yes, oh yes!"

His lips wandered over her silk skin, kissing and touching along the way, sucking first one breast then the other into his mouth. Pushing them together with his wet fingers while his tongue wreaked havoc on both. Then, just when she thought she would die of the pleasure, he continued his stroll south. Moving as if he had all the time in the world, when Sophie was feeling as if she were about to spontaneously combust at any minute.

The man was a demon to torture her with such sweet agony. Soon, she felt his hands on her legs, pushing them apart, and she held her breath in anticipation, as he kissed the insides of both thighs, ran his tongue through her curls, and finally plunged his tongue inside her.

"Oh, El! I can't take it!" She twisted beneath his cruel mouth, trying to free her hands, needing to participate in this assault, wanting to hold his hands to her. Then she clamped her legs around his shoulders. The slight pain in her ankle was a forgotten memory as she pushed against his hungry mouth, feeding him, loving him, wanting more of him.

"Please, El!" she begged, hoping he would understand before it was too late, before she took flight without him. He understood, because suddenly, the whole impressive length of him was sliding deep inside her, stretching her, making room for himself and, as she so loved about him, demanding his place inside her.

Together they took to the skies as the release came down hard and heavy. Sophie bucked uncontrollably beneath him, as he held her to his body and absorbed the blows, pumping his essence inside her until he felt like nothing more than an empty vessel.

Leaving a sticky trail of juice across her midsection, he reached up and released the scarf knot that held her hands in place, then pulled the other scarf off her head. "Thank you," he whispered against her shoulder. "Thank you for trusting me," he muttered, before falling asleep on top of her.

Sophie lay there for several minutes more, trying to understand what her senses were telling her was the truth. That El was thanking her for more than just the sexual experience they'd shared…he was thanking her for something profoundly more. But she had no idea what.

Chapter 17

The next morning, Eliot had a lunch basket prepared, and they spent a large part of the day in Fuller State Park. Eliot had to change his plans a little, because he'd planned for them to hike the park. But it didn't take long to figure out Sophie wouldn't be hiking anywhere.

So when they got out of the car, Eliot carried her on his back. "I'm such an idiot," he said, climbing a slight incline to find a place to picnic for lunch.

"No, you're not. I thought once the cast came off, my ankle would be one hundred percent."

"No, I should have known that a newly healed ankle would be weak."

Once they reached the top of the incline, Eliot sat her down. Opening the basket, he brought out a blanket and spread it on the ground. Then he lifted her and sat her on the blanket.

Digging through the basket, he pulled out two well-wrapped egg salad sandwiches and two bottles of iced tea.

"Thank you, Dale," El said, biting into his sandwich. He

shook his head. "Still don't know why you thought that was so funny."

She smiled. "I don't know. I guess because they kinda look like 'em, and then with that cowboy garb they were wearing, it was just too much." The wind blew by, and she lifted her face to it. "This is nice."

He smiled. "I'm sure any day you get to spend out of that kitchen is probably nice." He took another bite of his sandwich. "You work too hard."

"Not hard enough," she muttered. "Even with all our new clients, we are still barely making ends meet."

"Because of the new equipment?"

"Yes," she answered. "It's like a catch-22. We can't service new clients without the new equipment, but by buying the equipment we sink that much more in debt." She frowned, remembering something. "By the way, why haven't you cashed any of your payroll checks?"

"What?"

"I was balancing the books, and I realized we have a lot more money in the account than we should. When I traced it I discovered it's because none of your payroll checks have cleared."

"Hmm, that's odd," he said, but he didn't look as if he found it the least bit odd. "I'll contact my bank and check it out."

She frowned. "You do that. I won't accept your charity, El."

"What are you talking about?"

"You not cashing the checks because you know we're struggling. I appreciate the sentiment, but I won't accept it. I wouldn't have hired you if I didn't think we could afford you."

El continued to eat his sandwich without responding.

Later than evening, instead of going out they had dinner at the bed-and-breakfast with Roy and Dale, and another couple visiting from Indiana. The husband had been offered a job in the area, and the couple was doing what the wife called "a little reconnaissance."

It turned out that Roy and Dale were as fun as their names. They shared the easy banter of a couple who had been together a long time, telling humorous stories about when they were getting the inn up and running. It had been in pretty bad shape then—but you wouldn't know it to see the place now, Sophie thought.

For a moment, she allowed herself to daydream about opening a little bed-and-breakfast with El. She would manage the place, and he would cook for the guests, and they would spend their nights curled against each other until the end of time.

That Sunday, El completely changed his plans. Instead of driving down to the Mammoth Caves in Kentucky to do a little spelunking, they did a driving tour of the city. Down Beale Street, a drive-by of Alex Haley's boyhood home by AutoZone Park, and various other local tourist attractions. They laughed easily together and talked about everything they saw. But, Sophie did not miss the way El always deflected questions about himself.

Finally, as it was getting late, they decided to head back to the bed-and-breakfast for dinner. "I would say I'm sorry the weekend didn't go exactly as you planned, but I'm not sorry we came. I loved it. And not to sound ungrateful, but whatever gave you the idea I would want to go hiking through a park and *spelunking* in a cave?"

"You don't like spelunking?"

"Don't know, never tried it. I just wonder what made you think I wanted to try it."

"Your natural curiosity and competitive spirit would be perfect for the sport. You really should try it. I think you'll love it."

She looked up at him shyly beneath her lashes. "Maybe next time?"

He smiled. "Definitely next time."

She smiled and settled back into the car seat, hoping there would be a next time.

That evening while El was showering, Sophie lay in the bed watching TV, when she heard his cell phone ringing from his pants pocket. She considered not answering it. It wasn't the first time she'd heard it ring and not answered it. She didn't feel they knew each other well enough for her to take those kinds of liberties. But the way he'd gone out of the way to take his call the other day still bothered her.

So against her better judgment, she answered. "Hello?"

The person on the other end hesitated a moment. "Hello?"

"Who is this?"

"This is Steve. Who are you?"

She quickly turned the phone off. She shouldn't have answered it. She shouldn't have answered it. As she heard the shower stop, she shoved the phone back down in El's pants pocket.

He came out of the bathroom a few minutes later, toweling himself dry. Something about her face must have given her away, because he immediately asked, "What's wrong?"

"Nothing." She tried to keep her attention on the phone and away from his probing eyes.

The cell phone rang again, and Sophie felt her heart skip a beat. She pretended to ignore the ringing as El answered the phone, still watching her.

"Hello? Oh, hey, Steve."

She continued to watch the TV until she couldn't stand it any longer and her eyes darted to his. He was still watching her.

"Oh really?…I see." He sat down on the end of the bed and had a short conversation with the man. Finally, he turned to her, and she expected some kind of reprimand for crossing boundaries. But instead he said, "Sophie, if you are going to answer my phone, at least take a message." He gave her a quick kiss, then stood and, walking back into the bathroom, finished toweling himself off.

Eliot closed the bathroom door and leaned back against it. That was close. Thankfully, it had only been Steve. But what if it had been his uncle calling? Or someone who called him by his real name? One phone call could ruin everything.

Here he was spending an enjoyable weekend with the woman he loved—and he was now certain he loved Sophie—and one phone call…just one…could take her away from him.

What a mess he'd made of all this. And now it was up to him to undo the mess. When he'd started out it was a simple proposition: find out what he could, possibly even steal the recipe book. Things his uncle had expected from him for years.

But when he was with Sophie, he was a different man. Less the man molded by his uncle's harsh treatment and more the man his parents had started building with their love and quiet support. They never got to finish the job, but the core of that boy was still in his heart. And he knew this because that part of him appreciated the kindness and goodness in Sophie and Mae.

He'd put it off too long, and now time was truly running out. He had to find a way to undo his deception without Sophie ever finding out what his original intentions were. They were so right for each other in so many ways. He finally found the right woman—why did it have to be under these circumstances?

Chapter 18

Later that week, Eliot was carrying boxes of books and magazines Sophie had kept with her at the store into her small house, a three-bedroom, brick bungalow. "This is nice," he said. This was his first visit to her home.

"Thanks," she said, pulling her suitcase behind her. "It's good to be home. Hungry?"

"No thanks. I could go for a glass of water, though."

"Coming right up."

Eliot busied himself looking over her family pictures. Sophie with her brothers and sisters when they were children. Her parents, some smaller children he assumed were nieces and nephews.

Soon Sophie returned with a tall glass of ice water. "You know, when I first read your résumé, I had the impression you were a bit of a snob. I thought, okay, he can probably cook great, but that's all he'll be good for. I must admit I was wrong. You are one hardworking brother," she said and laughed.

He sat on the end of her sofa. "Only when I know there is something in it for me."

She stepped between his thighs and wrapped her arms around his neck. "And what's in it for you?"

He nodded toward the hallway leading to the bedrooms. "We haven't christened your bed as a couple." A wide grin spread over his face.

But Sophie's serious expression never changed. "We never christened yours, either. In fact, I have no idea where you live."

Eliot's smile fell away. "It's nothing impressive. Just a room I'm renting while I'm in this area."

"And there's the other problem."

"What do you mean?"

"You have no intention of staying here. You are only here as long as it takes old grudges to be forgotten, and then you are returning to Houston."

"You don't know that."

"Don't I? You just said, you're only renting a room while you're in this area."

"Things change, Sophie. The circumstances of people's lives change all the time. Maybe I will get a more permanent place."

She backed out of his arms and crossed the room to her suitcase. "I can't build my life on maybe, El." Pulling the little cart, she went into the bedroom, and Eliot followed.

After a quick glance around the room, he picked up right where they left off. "What are you asking for here, Sophie? A commitment. That's fine. I can give you a commitment, but the details are still sketchy."

She lifted the suitcase up on the bed and unzipped it. "What is that supposed to mean?"

"It means I can tell you that I want a future with you, but I can't say for sure when that will be. There are things in my past I have to clean up first."

She huffed, "Jealous ex-lovers and their angry husbands, perchance?"

Eliot decided that was probably better than the truth. "That's part of it."

She started unpacking the suitcase. "Look, never mind. I'm sorry I brought it up. I'm not even sure why I brought it up."

He walked up behind her, placing his large hands on her small shoulders. "Because you are starting to fall for me just like I'm falling for you. And just like me, you're scared we are going to screw this up somehow."

She turned in his arms. "You're falling for me?"

"Hard."

"Then why not go ahead and find a more permanent place, or…you could move in here."

He smiled. "Thank you, sweetheart, but I want to unload my garbage and be rid of it forever. Not drag it to your front door."

She shook her head and returned to her unpacking. "You know, if anyone would've told me I would fall in love with a baker, I would've thought, cool, perfect fit, since I run a bakery. But I swear you are more complicated than a Chinese puzzle."

He laughed. "No, just a few scrambled pieces that need to be put back in place."

Later that night, after her featherbed had been quite thoroughly christened, El lay sound asleep on his stomach, one arm hanging off the bed. His long, lean form took up most of the space. She had always thought she had a big bed, until she'd seen this man in it.

Her eyes ran over his outline in the shadows, the dip of his lower back and the curve of his perfectly shaped butt. Long, muscular legs that seemed to go on forever. He was an exceptionally fine man, she thought, and she did love him. But it was hard to just let go and enjoy the pleasure of being in love when you didn't know much about your lover.

After the phone call in Memphis, Sophie had begun to do a mental inventory of just how much she knew about El. And she was shocked to realize that most of what she did know about him had come from the agency he worked for and not from the man himself.

So, short of suspending her entire thought process, she was beginning to have questions. The fact that it had taken her this long to ask those questions was a testament to just how far gone she was over this man.

She ran her hand over his exposed back. It was hard not to be.

Just look at him! If she'd built him from scratch, she couldn't have done any better. He was perfect for her, in looks and temperament, even the way he fit inside her body seemed custom-made. So, why did she now get a queasy feeling in the pit of her stomach every time his phone rang?

It was a hard pill to swallow, but Sophie had to acknowledge that after nine weeks knowing this man, she did not know a single person in his world, and he seemed to like it that way.

Suddenly, his large hand moved, feeling its way across the bed. It hooked around her waist and slid her against his side. Then all was quite again.

Sophie yawned, sleepy and frustrated, and still no closer to an answer regarding her relationship with El. Deciding there was no need in torturing herself any longer on something that obviously would not be resolved that night, she nestled down against his side and went to sleep.

The next day, the milk delivery truck driver had spilled a whole crate on the sidewalk while unloading the truck. He'd taken it off the invoice, of course, but the mess on the sidewalk was a smelly invitation to nature's critters, especially given the extreme heat they had been experiencing lately.

She and Mae had taken on the task of scrubbing down the front walk, and Sophie thought this was as good a time as any to talk to her grandmother, while they were out of earshot of everyone else.

"Grandma, how long did you and Granddad know each other before you married?"

Mae stopped pushing her broom through the soapy water on the sidewalk, pausing to think. "Oh, Lord, that was so long ago. Let me think." She began pushing the brush again. "Maybe ten or eleven months."

Sophie's eyes widened in surprise. "That's less than a year!"

"Yes, that sounds about right." Mae nodded and continued scrubbing with her broom.

"You had a forty-year marriage with someone you'd known less than a year."

Mae nodded, not seeing what was so impressive about that. "When you find the right person, ain't no sense in wasting a bunch of time courting when you could be getting to the business of building your life together."

"How do you know when you've found the right person?"

Mae smiled. "Because even though you've only known him a short time, seems like you've known him forever, feels like he's always been a part of your life. Usually, those are the ones. The ones that fit right even *before* you meet them."

Sophie was trying to process that as Mae continued: "El has something riding him hard, Sophie. Don't know what it is, but there's something he don't want the rest of us to know about. I was thinking it had to do with why such a big-shot pastry chef would take a job here. But if you are talking this way, then it must be something else." She shook her head. "Don't know what it is. But, he's a good man in the middle where it matters, even if the edges are a little tattered."

"I know, Grandma. It's just he's so secretive about his life." She glanced at her grandmother. "I thought maybe...maybe he's married."

Mae frowned. "No, not married. That's not it."

"How can you be so sure?"

"The way he is with you. I'm seen my fair share of cheating husbands. They're real careful, trying to pace themselves, trying not to draw attention. But El doesn't act like that. For one, he's not careful at all; he hounds you like that ol' collie I had." She stopped bushing the broom, bracing her hand on her hip. "You remember him, don't you? The one that was always humping the pillows and whatever else he could get his paws around."

Sophie burst into laughter. "I remember him."

She nodded knowingly. "That's El. Not careful at all."

Sophie shook her head, thinking of how much she loved this woman. And how empty her life would have been if she'd abandoned her like the rest of the family.

Mae started pushing the brush again. "Always in behind you." She shook her head. "Trying to do the natural. No, that's no cheating man." She walked to the dry portion of the sidewalk and picked up a half-empty bucket of water. Tossing it across the soapy mess they'd made, she continued her scrubbing.

Sophie walked to her grandmother and kissed the top of her head. "You can always make me feel better."

"That's why I'm here," Mae said, matter-of-factly and continued with her chore.

Chapter 19

Eliot was typing away on his computer. It had been almost three months since he'd first taken on the persona of El the Baker, and in his absence the work load had built up beyond belief. Kara, his assistant had kept him apprised of the most pressing matters, and he worked from home in the late evenings and early mornings, but he was still facing a morning filled with appointments, and department heads needing to talk to him about one thing or another.

It seemed to him that every few minutes Kara was running into the office with an armload of documents, needing review or signatures. And in the midst of all the madness, Eliot could not stop himself from occasionally glancing toward the window. Where was Sophie right now? What was she doing? What was going on in the store? he wondered.

The life he lived here seemed thousands of miles away from that world, and yet it was roughly an hour's drive. He'd taken the day off, using the excuse of having to return to Houston to check on his home there, and in truth, he had gone to Houston over the weekend to check on the real Alberto Montagna, who was healing nicely. But Eliot didn't know how long that would last. As he was leaving the hospital room, a beautiful woman was entering. She looked decidedly nervous, and it didn't take much for him to realize this was the mistress and the cause of Alberto's predicament. Glancing at her pretty face, Eliot found himself considering Sophie's question once more. *Was she worth it?* With one final glance back at Alberto, wrapped in bandages, his whole world turned completely upside down, Eliot knew he'd given the right answer.

He hurried through the piles or work, delegating as much as possible, which was not his style. But he had no intention of staying away from Sophie longer than he had to. His cell phone rang and he snatched it out of his pocket. "Hello?"

"Eliot, hi, it's Steve. Got a minute?"

"Sure."

"Better yet, where are you?"

"At the headquarters in Memphis."

"Wanna have lunch?"

"Sorry, I have too much to do."

"I'll bring it by there. I really need to talk to you, and I don't want to do it on a phone if I can help it."

"Understood. I expect to be here all day."

"Great. See you this afternoon."

Eliot was a little surprised by the fact that he had not seen his uncle all morning, but he had so much to do and the hours went so quickly it was lunchtime before he knew it.

His desk phone rang and he answered. It was Kara announcing Steve, so Eliot made some space on his crowded desk. Steve had brought subs from his favorite place.

As he took a bite, he smiled to himself.

"What's that look about?" Steve asked.

"Just thinking. I used to think this was a pretty good lunch. But Mae Mayfield cooks these large lunches for the employees every day, and I guess I've gotten a little spoiled by it."

Steve frowned. "I can order in something different, if you like."

Eliot shook his head. "No, I'm not complaining, just an observation."

"You've gotten attached to them, haven't you?"

Eliot sighed. "Afraid so."

Steve wiped his mouth, and pushed his sandwich to the side. "That's going to make what I have to tell you even harder."

"Just say it, Steve."

"You know how you asked me to let you know anything about your uncle acting without your knowledge against the bakery? Well, I think he does have something in the works, although I'm not sure what that is. But in the processing of getting that information, I came across something more troubling."

"Just spit it out."

"Your uncle has been having you followed."

"What?!"

"He's been having you tailed for the past two weeks or so. At least, I don't think it's been any longer than that."

"Why?"

"Apparently, he's become suspicious of why you have not acted against the bakery. And I'm pretty certain he knows about your relationship with the girl. The report said something about a weekend here?"

Eliot nodded in confirmation. "Yeah, we came to town to celebrate her getting her cast off." He frowned thoughtfully. "So he's decided to try and go around me, huh?"

"Looks that way. Just wanted you to know." He glanced around the office. "Quite honestly, I'm not entirely comfortable talking here, but I wanted to get this to you as soon as possible."

"Thanks, Steve, I appreciate that. Just keep me updated on anything you hear."

The two men finished up their lunch and discussed a few other issues that Eliot had been neglecting during his time in Selmer. Then Steve left, but the warning he'd given had been taken to heart.

Eliot knew he was on borrowed time. No one knew his uncle better than he did, and he knew the old man would not wait forever. In fact, he should have considered the possibility that he was being followed. That was exactly what he would have expected Carl Fulton to do. But he'd allowed himself to fill his head with only thoughts of Sophie, and that was dangerous. In order to protect her, he would have to stay sharp and focused. It was the only way to stand against his uncle.

He spent the rest of the day and part of the evening clearing his desk, but by the time he was preparing to leave that night there was still more work to be done. He sat back in his chair and looked at the stacks of unfinished business. They would have to wait, he thought, glancing at his watch. If he left now, he could get back to Selmer before Sophie fell asleep, which was usually around eleven.

"That's the cost of neglect."

He glanced up at the man standing in the doorway. "Wondered when you would show up."

"I have a job to do, as well. And unlike you, I'm diligent in mine."

"Why are you having me followed?"

Carl tilted his head in confusion. "Followed? Wherever did you get that idea?"

"Don't bother denying it."

Carl walked into the room. "What's the status on this bakery thing? How close are you to closing them down? I can't afford to have you out of the office much longer."

Eliot just stared at the other man.

"Fine, have it your way. But I always win, Eliot. If you haven't figured out at least that much by now, I guess I've been wasting my time."

As he walked out of the office, Eliot knew the day of reckoning was at hand. From the moment he became aware of just what kind of man his uncle was, he'd known that one day the two of them would lock horns and battle until one of them fell. He'd thought the battle would eventually be over the executive office. He couldn't see his uncle giving it up without a fight. He'd never imagined it would be over a woman. But then again, he never imagined he'd meet a woman like Sophie.

An hour later, in his study at home, Carl poured a glass of scotch, settled into his favorite recliner and placed a call.

"Hello?" a deep voice on the other end answered.

"Is he still there?"

"Yes, sir."

"Good. I need you to use some of your contacts to check out that girl's background. Her family. Make sure she doesn't have any skeletons in the closet. No crazy ex-husbands or kids."

"Yes, sir. But wouldn't you rather I have someone else do that so I can stay on Mr. Wright?"

Carl chuckled. "Don't worry. Mr. Wright's not going anywhere anytime soon. He's got too much of me in him. He'd temporarily forgotten his priorities, but he's back on track now. Just go make sure this girl is clean."

Carl hung up the phone and sat back in the plush recliner. So Eliot had fallen in love. Somehow Carl had not seen it coming. He knew the boy had had affairs, but nothing serious. But now he was putting his life and goals on hold for…a woman. And a country girl, at that.

Carl shook his head and took another sip of his scotch. Carl had never fallen into that trap. There had been women, plenty of them. But none worth distracting him from his goals—to make Fulton Foods the largest snack foods and pastry provider in the greater Memphis area. And he'd done it, too. He'd doubled the distribution, doubled the profit and streamlined the production process. But it hadn't happened overnight, and it hadn't been easy. It had taken sacrifice, dedication and single-minded purpose. Things no married man could afford.

But, that kind of driving ambition had a price, as Carl well knew. He took another sip of scotch. By the time he began considering his own mortality he was well into his forties. But even then he felt he had plenty of time to build a family: a line of strong, fine boys and girls to take over the company. He found a nice, pliable woman, a schoolteacher from Jackson, and proposed to her. He had gotten to work trying to breed on her right away. But after almost six months, Carl began to wonder. Considering his family history, it was understandable. His father had been an only child, and throughout his childhood years Carl could count on one hand the number of children that had been born in the family. So, he had himself checked out and discovered his swimmers had some kind of genetic deficiency. There was a possibility that he could sire a child eventually, but the chances against it were greater. It was hard news to take, but Carl had never been a man to shy away from the truth.

He broke off his engagement to the schoolteacher, not seeing the point in marrying if he could not have children. He turned his attention to watching his sister's family. She'd been married only a few years, but already it was starting to look as if she, too, had the family curse. And then a few years later she got pregnant with Eliot. And no one was happier to see his sister give birth to a healthy baby boy than Carl, because it meant he had an heir.

But like his father before him, Carl didn't believe in giving anything away. No, whatever you got in life had to be earned, even if you were destined for it. So he watched in disdain as his sister and that pantywaist husband of hers coddled the boy and damn near ruined him.

Then the unthinkable had happened. Carl had lost his only sibling in a senseless car crash. But as if in answer to his prayers, the boy had been spared. Of course, his idiot brother-in-law had left that will stating that Eliot was to go to his useless sister, but Carl wasn't about to let a little thing like a will come between him and his heir.

So, he'd hired the best lawyers money could buy and fought tooth and nail for custody and won. Taking the boy in was a decision Carl had never regretted. He'd made him a man. Toughened him up, gotten rid of the wimpy mama's boy he'd been when he first arrived. And turned him into a purpose-driven shark…at least, that's what he'd been until recently. But, now, his head was being turned by some woman, and Carl was determined to know as much about her as possible. Once he had all the facts, then he would decide whether to welcome her into the family fold…or break her in half.

Chapter 20

Everything seemed to fall back into a routine the following week. Then Eliot arrived home from Sophie's place early one morning, and was about to shower and change to head out to the bakery when the phone rang.

He almost didn't answer it, fearing it was some catastrophe at the office he did not want to deal with at the moment. But he did answer. "Hello?"

"Good, I caught you."

"What is it, Uncle Carl? I'm in a hurry."

"Were you still planning to attend that industry convention in New York next week? They're always held in June."

Eliot sat down hard on the sofa. With everything else going on, he'd completely forgotten about the annual industry convention he usually attended. "Can't this year."

"Why not?"

"Too much going on right now. Can't you get someone else to go?"

"There is no one else with your expertise or connections.

You've attended the International Dairy-Deli-Bakery Association's convention every year for the past ten years! You're the slated guest speaker, for goodness sake!"

"Fine! Fine, I'll go."

"Eliot, I don't like what I've been hearing lately about you and that Sophie Mayfield. How are you going to close her store when you're sleeping with the girl?"

Eliot's eyes narrowed. "What did you say?" Carl's sudden silence was all the confirmation of what Steve had told him that Eliot needed. He leaned forward. "I'm only going to say this once, Uncle Carl. I told you before I'll handle Mayfield Bakery, and I will. In my time, in my way. Are we clear?"

"If you don't, Eliot, I will."

"What's that supposed to mean?"

"I've had my attorney look into the contracts we have with Morningside and Centerfield. Turns out there is no early out option. It's hidden but legal. If I have to I will play that trump card."

"To what end?"

"You just make sure it doesn't come to that."

"Uncle Carl, I'm warning you. Stay away from Mayfield."

"You're warning me? *You're* warning *me?* Who the hell do you think you are?"

"I'm what you've made me."

"Cut the crap! You went down there for one purpose and one purpose only. Here we are months later, and you are still dragging your heels."

"It's complicated."

"No more complicated than anything else you've done. I've watched you take a competitor apart in a matter of days. As far as I can see the only real difference this time is that girl!"

"I'm only going to say this once again. *I'm* handling the Mayfield thing, not *you!*"

"That woman's got you thinking with the wrong head. You better decide where your loyalties lie, boy. You can't have it both ways. Either you're with me or against me!"

"We both know this is not about the Mayfield Bakery, Uncle Carl. You are trying to use this to control me, like you've always done. But, it's not going to work this time. This time, you may be surprised by who comes out on top."

Carl laughed. "So…there it is. After all these years of feeding you, clothing you, sheltering you and nurturing you, there's the gratitude."

"No one asked you to take me in!"

"What was I supposed to do, leave you with that aunt of yours, so she could continue to ruin you?!"

Eliot sighed, wondering how the conversation had deteriorated to this point so quickly. "I've got to get out of here—and don't worry, I'll go to the convention. But mark my words, Uncle Carl, if you come anywhere near that bakery…you'll regret it."

Carl was silent for so long, Eliot almost hung up. "I'm getting a little tired of you threatening me, Eliot. I raised you like a son, for one purpose. Fulton. I'm not about to let you ruin that now."

Then the phone went dead. Eliot hung up, but he knew his uncle too well to assume that was the end of the conversation. He immediately dialed Steve's cell phone.

"Hello?"

"Hey, it's Eliot. You heard anything about what my uncle may be up to?"

"No, why?"

"Just a feeling. Something he said about a clause in the contracts of our former clients."

"Hmm. I'll check it out and let you know what I find."

"Thanks, Steve. Look, I'm going to be in New York for a few days, but keep me up to date. The old man's up to something, and I want to know what it is."

When he arrived at the bakery almost an hour later, he was greeted at the sidewalk by Sophie. She looked bright, and cheery and beautiful.

"You left before I woke up this morning," she said. "I didn't have a chance to give you this."

She pulled a card from behind her back. "Happy anniversary!" She glanced over her shoulder at the empty storefront. "Read it before you go in."

"What anniversary?" Eliot asked, peeling the card open. He quickly read the short script and her personalized note at the bottom. "Three months?"

She glanced back once more, and then threw her arms around his neck and place a brief kiss on his lips. "Three months since the day you came to work here."

He chuckled. "Baby, I'm pretty sure most employees do not get three-month anniversary cards." He opened his car door, and tossed the card on the seat. "But, thanks for the thought."

"And I'm sure most *employees* don't *perform* as well as you do." She winked and turned to go back inside.

"Okay, I just went from feeling recognized and appreciated to cheap and sleazy," he said, following her inside.

She stopped in the doorway and gave him a sly smile. "If it's any consolation, you're not cheap."

Watching his face as the comment hit, she raced inside, and he was right behind her. They were both still laughing as they entered the kitchen.

Later than day, they sat around the preparation table talking and getting the latest town gossip from Dante and Lonnie. As Mae served up a lunch of fried chicken, Eliot realized he was starting to prefer this world to his old one. Even Wayne, sitting opposite him and currently biting into a chicken leg, was becoming tolerable. On some level, they'd made their peace about who Sophie belonged to and managed to work together pretty well. Sophie was helping Mae, placing cans of soda pop at everyone's elbow, then bringing over a piping-hot bowl of fresh buns he'd prepared right before they all sat down. Eliot was starting to see them as the family he'd never had, and the idea of his uncle hurting any of them was unacceptable.

Later that day, in one of those rare moments when he found himself alone in the kitchen, he saw Sophie passing by on her way to the office. He grabbed her around the waist and pulled her back against him. "So, how are we going to celebrate our anniversary?"

"Oh, I have it all planned out. I call it the one-*D* package."

"One-*D*. Is that suppose to be an upgrade from my three-*B* package?"

"Oh, no, I couldn't improve on the 'three-*B* package.' This is totally different."

"Okay, let's hear it."

"Dinner."

"Dinner? That's it?"

"Yes…but I'm cooking it."

"Oh, that *is* different."

"See, told you. In fact—" she glanced at the clock on the wall "—I'm cutting out of here a little early just so I have time to get everything ready."

"What are we having?"

"It's a surprise." She smiled seductively. "So is dessert."

As she wiggled out of his arms and went into the office, Eliot turned back to sugaring the cookies. But his mind was on the disturbing dream he'd had at least a week ago, the memory of which had never faded.

Tonight, he was going to tell Sophie that he was leaving town. While he was away, he would work out a plan for dealing with his uncle once and for all.

Chapter 21

"Well?" Sophie watched him with bright eyes as he took a second bite of the chocolate soufflé.

Eliot smiled. "Very good."

"Does it taste like yours?"

He frowned. "Sophie, it doesn't have to taste like mine to be good."

She frowned back. "So, it *doesn't* taste like yours."

He took another bite. "As flattering as that is, I think you are underestimating yourself. This is excellent," he said.

She toyed with hers. "Whatever."

Eliot sat his fork down beside his plate and wiped his mouth. Sophie had cooked a delicious and simple dinner of homemade Chicken Alfredo and steamed broccoli. But dessert was the real main course, and she'd spent the day working on a perfect chocolate soufflé. Apparently, she'd been trying to re-create something Eliot had created for a customer. The soufflé was good, not quite of the quality he'd produced, but he wasn't about to tell her that.

He took her hand in his. "Are you always this hard on yourself?"

"What do you mean?"

"Sometimes it seems as if you have to excel at everything you try. You don't cut yourself any slack for mistakes."

Her eyes narrowed suspiciously. "It's that bad?"

"No." He laughed. "The soufflé is fine. I'm talking about you—Sophie Mayfield."

She continued to toy with the food on her plate. "I don't like to fail. What's so bad about that?"

"The way you treat yourself when you do." He nodded toward her plate. "Here you spent the whole day cooking this wonderful meal. But because you think it's not perfect, or what you perceive as perfect, you are not able to enjoy it. Just seems like such a waste."

She shrugged. "I don't know. I just hate to lose. It's embarrassing."

"And you hate being embarrassed or humiliated."

"It's got to be one of the worst feelings in the world."

"Well, you don't have to worry about being embarrassed if you ever serve this soufflé to anyone else. It's very good."

She stood to collect the dishes, and Eliot stood to help her. "No, that's okay, I got it." She gestured toward her small living room. "Can you put some music on?"

He went into her living room. Digging through her stacks and stacks of CDs, he decided exactly what he would give her for Christmas…an MP3 player. He pulled out an Amy Winehouse CD and popped it in.

Sophie came back into the room carrying mugs of coffee. She placed them on the coffee table and, folding her leg beneath her, sat down on the couch.

He sat down beside her. "Listen, I have to go take care of some family business, and I'm going to be away for a few days."

"Oh?" she asked with interest.

He simply nodded and sipped his coffee.

"El, you never say anything about your family. Are they in Texas?"

"Actually, Memphis."

"Really? Is that why you took the job here? To be closer to your family?"

"Not exactly." He took another sip of the coffee, trying to find a way to change the subject. He glanced around the room. "This is cozy. Lived here long?"

When she didn't answer, he turned and looked at her.

"What are you keeping from me, El? I know you and I can feel you're keeping something from me."

He shrugged. "I have some pretty funky family dynamics. Nothing I want to talk about. Can we leave it there for now?"

She leaned forward until her nose was almost touching his. "Sure, but understand something. I better not find out you have a wife and kids stashed away somewhere. Because if I ever found out you were married…"

Unable to resist, he closed the rest of the distance between them and kissed her lips. "What are you going to do?" he teased, feeling relief. At least he was innocent of that charge.

"I will cut your balls off while your sleep."

Eliot sat back in wide-eyed horror, and then she burst into laughter.

He shook his head. "You're scary."

"Only if you have a family hidden away somewhere."

Later that night, they lay with limbs entwined in her soft, feathery bed after making love. Eliot could feel Sophie's heart-beat slowing against his chest, and he knew she would be asleep soon.

At least he thought so, until she said, "How long will you be gone?"

"No more than three days."

She ran her hand through his curly chest hair. "How am I supposed to live without this for three days?"

"I was just thinking the same thing."

"Hurry back to me."

"I will. Sophie, about what you were saying earlier. About my never talking about my family."

"Yes?"

"I didn't have a very good childhood, and I try not to think about it too much."

She turned on her side to look at him. "Sometimes talking about things helps you to work through them."

Amidst the dim light, he looked into her concerned brown eyes. "I'm not sure I'm ready to work through this."

He frowned thoughtfully. "Things have gotten even more complicated lately, and I just have some loose ends to tie up. When I do, then I'll be able to tell you everything."

Her mouth twisted in a sarcastic expression.

"What?"

"Nothing." She folded her arms, and turned over to look up at the ceiling.

Eliot propped himself up on one elbow. "What?"

She sighed. "I dated this guy a while back, who tried to convince me he was some kind of undercover operative, as if I was an idiot or something. He would give me all these emotion-filled confessions about how there was so much he wanted to tell me and couldn't, yada, yada, yada."

Eliot laughed. "Is that what I sound like?"

She shrugged. "I'm just saying it sounds a lot like you're in the Mafia or something, all this clandestine stuff about painful memories, and—" she made air quotes with her hands "—*family business* that takes you away for days at a time—but you can't tell me where you're going or what you're doing."

"Hmmm. I see your point."

She suddenly flipped over to face him again. "And the other guy I was dating—guess where he was going when he left on a 'secret mission'?"

Eliot frowned. "Home to his family?"

She poked his forehead with her index finger. "You guessed it!"

Eliot covered her body, bearing her back down on the bed. "I'm not married, Sophie. I swear, I'm not married." He lifted his right hand. "And if I'm lying may God let my balls *fall* off, before you ever have a chance to *cut* them off."

Sophie looked over his shoulder. "You hear that, God?"

Eliot laughed and kissed her neck. Being in this position with her made him already half-aroused. He shifted, lifting one of her legs higher on his hip. It was his favorite position with her, because it allowed him to sink deep inside her body. "There's only one, Sophie," he whispered against the silky-soft skin of her shoulder. "For me, there is only you."

Sophie moaned in satisfaction. "I hope so, baby…" She groaned, reaching beneath the covers to wrap her hands around his testicles. "I do so love these guys."

Eliot laughed. Taking both her hands, he lifted them over her head, as he plowed into her body relentlessly, trying to tell her with his flesh what he already knew in his soul. There was only one woman for him, and she was it.

When El left the next morning, Sophie tried to play the part of the casual lover, but as he moved toward the door, she realized she would not see him for three full days, and she could not stop herself from rushing to him and wrapping her arms around him.

"Come back to me, fast," she said against his shoulder.

He kissed the top of her head. "I will." And then he was gone.

Sophie tried to occupy herself with running the store, but all day she kept glancing up, expecting to see El somewhere in the area. When she returned home that night, she didn't cook dinner, which would have just reminded her she was alone. Instead, she fixed a bowl of cereal and curled up in front of the television.

Just as she stepped out the shower around nine, the phone rang. She scrambled across the room, hoping, praying. "Hello?"

"What are you wearing?"

Her heart soared. "A wet towel."

"Ooh, perfect timing. Take it off."

She let the towel fall to the floor. He must have heard the swooping noise as it fell, because he said, "Now lay down on the bed."

Feeling her heartbeat accelerate, she climbed into the bed, still holding the cordless phone against her ear.

"Do you miss me?"

"Yes," she said in a stilted voice. "Every minute of the day."

"Good, that's what I wanted to hear, because I've been going crazy without you." His own breathing grew heavier by the moment, his voice deepening with lust. "I keep seeing these pictures in my head."

"What pictures?" She licked her dry lips.

"You—the first time I saw you in the back room of the bakery. Remember?"

"Yes."

"I close my eyes and I see it so clearly, you stroking yourself and calling my name. Those beautiful brown legs wide open, begging me to come inside. Those sweet, plump breasts needing the kind of love and attention only I can give them."

"Yes, El, yes…I remember," she moaned, her fingers inching down her midsection as he painted the vivid memory for her.

"You were like something out of a dream, and all I could think about was plunging as far inside you as I could go, and when I finally did…"

"Yes?" Her fingers toyed with her clit, her mind trying to stay focused on his words, on his voice, as she remembered exactly what it felt like to have him deep inside her.

"You closed around me like a new glove, so sweetly snug and tight."

"Yes, oh, yes, I remember."

"Your hot juices flowing over me, even through the condom I could feel your hot juice burning through me."

The words were fading away, as Sophie's attention centered on her own body. If she concentrated she could almost feel his heavy weight on top of her, holding her thighs open for him in that commanding way of his while he worked himself deeper and deeper inside her.

As if reading her mind, he said, "Can you feel that, baby?"

Sophie did feel it, the pressure building. She squeezed a hardened nipple as she imagined his mouth closing around one of her breasts. "Oh, El, I need you so much—hurry!"

She heard his groan of release through the phone and dropped the receiver as her orgasm washed over her. It didn't last long, because she could not manipulate her body the way El could, causing her release to last forever, making her climax over and over again.

She picked up the phone and could hear his harsh breath on the other end. "El?"

"Yeah, baby?"

"Hurry home to me."

"Believe me, sweetheart, I'm trying."

Chapter 22

When Sophie unlocked the front door of the bakery that morning, she noticed the big, silver sports sedan sitting at the curb but thought nothing of it.

As she entered the store and began turning on lights, she was surprised to see the door swing open and an older man follow her inside.

She was slightly wary, given his stern expression. "Can I help you?"

"I certainly hope so. My name is Carl Fulton, owner of Fulton Foods."

Sophie's eyes widened in surprise. She didn't know if she should shake hands and introduce herself or demand he leave her store. She decided on the former. "Sophie Mayfield, nice to meet you." She came forward with her hand extended, but he completely ignored it.

"I know who you are. Let me get straight to the point." He glanced around the store. "We both know you are in no position to compete with my company, but for some fool reason you've decided to try. You've been bidding on—and even winning—a few of my clients. But you won't be able to maintain them, and they will eventually come back to me. So to save us both some trouble, I have come to hear your demands."

"What?" Sophie was too flabbergasted to form more than the one-word response.

"I know several very respectful offers have been made to acquire your operation, and you have repeatedly turned them down. So, what is it that you want?"

Slowly, the confusion was being replaced with anger. "Well, Mr. Fulton, if you know those offers were rejected, what makes you think I would change my mind now?"

"Three reasons." He held up his fingers. "One, I will allow you to set your own terms. Two, you have no choice. Three, to save your business."

"Let's go with number two. What do you mean I have no choice?"

He smirked, and Sophie thought his face looked vaguely familiar although she couldn't quite place it. He reached inside his jacket pocket and pulled out a form. "If we cannot settle on terms today, I will file this claim *today*." He handed over the papers, and Sophie sat her keys and purse on the counter to accept the papers.

She quickly glanced at them. It was a document stating Fulton Foods was suing a variety of businesses, all of them former Fulton clients that had just signed on with her. "I don't understand."

"There is a clause in our contracts that stipulates certain terms. By signing with you, these clients violated those terms. I plan to sue each of them for breach of contract."

It was all beginning to click into place. By suing those clients, they would have no choice but to abandon her. Considering the debt she'd taken on to buy new equipment and supplies for the business, she would be deeper in the hole than ever. But there was something else, she hadn't even considered until he spoke again.

"By the time the media gets finished with this story—and I'll make sure they know about it—the name of your little bakery will be synonymous with *lawsuit,* and no one will want to do business with you." He chuckled. "You'll be lucky if you can keep your walk-in customers."

Sophie tossed the papers at his chest. He grabbed them and tucked them neatly back in his jacket pocket.

"You would do this over a handful of contracts?" She gestured to the store. "You just said we could never compete with you, so why do this?"

"Because this bakery is becoming a thorn in my side, young lady. And more importantly, you, personally, are becoming a considerable threat to the future of my business!"

"How could I—"

"Eliot Wright! Know the name?"

She shook her head in confusion.

He twisted his mouth in annoyance. "Maybe not. Your new baker—what's his name?"

"What business of yours is that?"

"He's my nephew! That's what!"

She shook her head in confusion. The man had apparently gone off the deep end. "That's impossible."

"Is it? Ask him. Oh, that's right, you can't. He's out of town right now."

Sophie felt the first butterflies in her stomach. "That doesn't prove anything."

During his tirade, Mae and Lonnie had come in the door behind him.

"Sophie? What's going on?" Mae asked, watching Carl Fulton with concern.

"Just a business matter, Grandma." Sophie gestured for Carl to follow her, and she headed back to her office.

As they walked back to the office, she could see he was checking out the new equipment and setup. She hated taking him through the store and the kitchen, letting him see the whole of her modest operation, but she needed to complete this conversation. What he was saying was too disturbing to go unchecked.

Once they were in the office, she closed the door. "What does any of this have to do with El?"

"El?" He arched an eyebrow, and the butterflies in her stomach began to go crazy as she instantly recognized that face. "Is that the name he's using? I guess it makes sense. It was his childhood nickname. But his real name is Eliot Wright, and he is my nephew and my chief financial officer."

Sophie still didn't believe it. She couldn't believe it. "Then what is he doing working as a baker in my kitchen?"

Carl smiled. "Proving to me how clever he can be. He originally came here to do exactly what I'm doing today. But someone assumed he was your new baker, and seeing that your new baker was currently unavailable, El decided to take the opportunity to learn what he could about your business."

"You're lying!"

"Am I?" he sneered. "Then why do you look as if you are about to cry?"

She quickly looked away.

"And yes, I know you're sleeping with him." He shrugged, as if it meant little. "Eliot tells me everything."

Sophie sat down in her chair, not sure how much longer her legs would support her.

"Before you fall apart on me, let me explain. This situation can be easily rectified." He patted his jacket pocket. "These papers need never be filed. Your business can have a respectable end." He opened his arms. "All you have to do is name your terms. I will pay whatever you feel this little place is worth. You will make a tidy profit, and Eliot can come back to his real life."

She shook her head. "I don't believe you."

Carl sighed heavily. "Oh, good Lord! Are you really this dense?!"

Sophie watched as for the first time since he'd entered the front door of her bakery, his façade of indifference slipped. He cared a lot more about this deal than he was willing to admit.

Summoning all the strength she could, Sophie stood to her feet. "No."

"What?"

"No, thank you, Mr. Fulton. Although, I appreciate your

generous offer, I must reject it on the premise that you're full of crap."

His amber eyes narrowed on her face, and she knew in her gut that at least half of what he'd told her was true. "Think long and hard, young lady. You *do not* want to get into a war with me."

Because she was completely convinced he was right, Sophie said nothing in response. After a few minutes of staring her down, he finally turned and walked out of the office.

From the door of her office, Sophie could see that Wayne and Dante had also come in. Now, they all stood as the stranger stormed through the kitchen and out the front door. Then they all turned and looked at her for answers. She had none.

She gently closed the door and sat down in her chair. Then inspired by hurt, anger and the need for action, stood again and threw open the door.

"Everyone, come into the front, please." She moved through the kitchen to the front of the store. Once her small group was gathered, she gave a brief overview of what had just happened.

"That was Carl Fulton, the owner of Fulton Foods. He was here to make one last offer to buy the bakery. If we don't accept, he made it perfectly clear that he plans to destroy us." She glanced at her grandmother. "Grandma, for so long I thought I was acting on your behalf, but I guess a selfish part of me didn't want to sell for my own reasons. But if you say sell, I'll sell."

Mae's worn face took on a hard look. "I'd rather burn it to the ground than give it over to him." Her quiet voice was laced with steel.

Sophie nodded. "All right, then, that's settled. I don't know what is about to come our way, but something is. He's planning to sue his former clients that signed with us. I'm going to call our lawyers to see what our options are. We will continue with business as usual. Agreed?" Getting everyone's agreement, she nodded and started to return to her office and paused, remembering the hardest part. "There is something else."

As if they had been waiting for the other shoe to drop, everyone turned their full attention to her.

"Turns out our baker, El, is actually…Carl Fulton's nephew."

"What?!" Mae said, clutching her heart.

"Seems he was Fulton's spy, sent to determine how much of a threat we really were."

"I knew he was no good!" Wayne hissed.

Lonnie didn't say a word, but the devastated expression on her face said she understood the implications. Dante put his arm protectively around her, but his facial expression wasn't any less hurt.

As they all gave their commentary and exchanged information, Sophie drifted back to her office. She didn't want to hear Dante bragging about how he knew before anyone else, nor did she want to hear her grandmother trying to make excuses for him. She just wanted to be alone with her thoughts and her memories.

The last time they were together, she'd told him about the ex who pretended to be a spy, and all the while El really was a spy. She reminded herself, "His family business really was family business." She finally put her head down on the desk, and closed her eyes, as the exhaustion of the morning temporarily took her over.

A short while later, Lonnie knocked on the door with her purse. She'd left it on the front counter that morning, and now the cell phone was ringing. She dug out the cell phone and saw the name on the caller ID. Then she turned it off and returned it to the purse.

"Thanks, Lonnie," she said quietly before putting her head back down on the desk. She did not want to talk to El, or Eliot, or whoever the hell he was. Not now, and probably not ever.

Chapter 23

Almost two hours after Carl Fulton left the store, Sophie was still sitting at her desk, shell-shocked. It didn't make sense. It couldn't be true. El was...El. Her baker, her lover. There was no way the man she loved could be the nephew of her enemy.

Wayne knocked on the door, and she looked up. "You okay?"

She nodded, wishing she'd locked the door.

"Sophie...I wanted to tell you something, but I don't know if I should."

She tried to focus her scrambled mind on what Wayne was saying. "What is it?"

"I have a friend who's a busboy at Catalan's."

Her eyes narrowed on his face. "How convenient."

Wayne sighed. "I knew I shouldn't have said anything." He started to turn away.

"Wait, Wayne. What did you busboy friend say?"

He turned back to her. "He said the man we know as El didn't sound like their guy. And something else is weird—they called him Al, not El. It's a little thing, but I thought you should know." He turned and left the office.

Sophie watched his retreating back as he moved through the office. Wayne had never liked El, so she was not surprised that he would be eager to reinforce what Carl had said. But what if there was some truth to it? Wayne might be on to something.

Catalan's. That's where the answers were. She grabbed her keys and purse and headed toward the front door.

"Sophie?" Mae called to her.

She paused before heading out the door. "Grandma, I'm going to be out of the office for a few days. I just—I just need some time." She walked out of the store and climbed into her car.

She'd planned to drive home, make a reservation and then catch a plane to Houston. Instead, she just kept driving, and driving and driving. Stopping only for gas and food. She arrived in Houston close to six that night.

As she pulled into the parking lot of the five-star restaurant, she considered for the first time what she must look like dressed in her wrinkled jeans and a T-shirt. She'd just driven in these clothes for ten hours. She definitely did not look like a patron of the swanky restaurant. So she pulled out of the lot, and parked about a block away.

She'd come too far to leave without having her questions answered. She walked around to the back entrance and waited for one of the employees to come out. She waited about twenty minutes before the door opened and a waitress stepped out.

"Excuse me?" She cautiously approached the young woman. "I'm looking for Alberto Montagna. Do you know him?"

The lady nodded. "But he doesn't work here anymore. Got fired awhile ago."

Sophie fished in her purse for her wallet. "Can you tell me if this man is Alberto Montanga?" She held up a picture of her and El together, the one they'd taken at the restaurant in Memphis. She'd had it reduced to fit in her wallet.

The young woman looked at the picture, then back at Sophie's tired face. "Look, I don't want to get involved." She started to walk away.

"Please," Sophie called, hating that her voice was cracking, hating that the tears were forming. "Please, you have no idea how important this is." She sniffed, and held up the picture once more. "Just look at this, please."

The woman glanced at the picture, and then did a quick double take. She shook her head. "No, that's not Alberto." The waitress smiled at Sophie, obviously believing her answer was the one she wanted, but once she saw the tears begin to slide down her cheeks, she turned and quickly walked away.

Sophie slowly walked back to her car, climbed into the driver's seat, put on her seat belt and just sat there. Holding the small picture between both hands, she stared at the face of the man who'd claimed to be Alberto Montagna for over two months. The man who in fact worked for her competitor, was related to her competitor. The man who'd come to her store for the sole purpose of destroying her. Her lover was a complete stranger, and that realization was both heart-wrenching and terrifying at the same time.

About an hour later, she started the engine and began the long drive back to Selmer. She was exhausted in both mind and body, and she considered pulling in somewhere for the night several times, but she pushed on. By the time she pulled up in front of her home just before sunrise, she felt like a broken windup doll, all cried out and numb.

It was too early to call anyone, and she considered leaving a message on her grandmother's cell, but who knew where it was? Then still fully dressed, she crawled into her bed and fell into a deep, fortifying sleep. When she awoke later, it was dusk.

Too humiliated to face anyone, Sophie waited until the store closed for the evening, and then she used her key to let herself inside. For reasons she would not think about, she wanted to sleep in the first bed she shared with El, so she went straight to the back room and curled up in the middle of the twin bed.

Lying there, she replayed all the times they'd shared in this tiny room. All the things they'd told each other. She'd bared her soul, and he'd fed her a line of bull. And she'd fallen for it hook, line and sinker.

She tried to convince herself that everyone made mistakes, and that El was just a mistake she'd made. Problem was, he didn't feel like a mistake. Even now. Even though she felt deeply betrayed and devastated by what she'd learned, it was still hard to regret her time with him.

The next morning, when everyone started coming in, they were all surprised to see Sophie coming out of the back apartment dressed and ready to start the day. No one asked why she was there and she was grateful for that.

She threw herself into the work, spending most of the morning paying bills and talking on the phone with the store's lawyers. They were as vague as ever, and by the time she hung up Sophie was still unsure if Carl Fulton's claim would stand up in court, or if it was all just bluster to scare her. She did know the anger she'd seen in his eyes was real, and if he could not crush her through legal means, then he would find other ways to destroy her.

After Eliot stepped off the plane in Memphis, he called Kara to get an update on what had happened at his office over the last couple of days. By the time he reached his car, he was fuming.

Kara explained what she knew through office gossip and that was scary enough, but after talking to Steve and getting the full picture, El was terrified. *Damn that old man!*

He headed into town to confront Carl but then turned in the direction of Selmer. He needed to see Sophie's face, see what she knew, know what she was thinking.

He cursed himself for all the opportunities he'd had to tell her the truth and had held back instead. He could only imagine what Carl had said to her. He drove like a maniac, as if reaching her faster could somehow reduce any damage that had already been done.

Forty-five minutes later, he pulled up in front of the bakery and took a deep breath. It looked the same, at least from the outside. But what was he expecting? Some kind of apocalyptic evidence that his world had been destroyed?

He walked to the door and could see Mae behind the counter, but the sun's reflection on the glass window made it impossible to make out her facial expression. As he opened the door, he wished he'd stayed in the car.

The look on the older woman's face was like a punch in his

gut. He could only imagine what Sophie must be thinking. Slowly, he approached the counter. "Mama Mae, is Sophie here?"

She nodded, still looking at him with distrust and distain.

He turned toward the kitchen and paused. "I know what you must think of me, and I probably deserve it, but I love Sophie." He turned to look at her. "My love for her is real."

She stared at him for a long time, and then turned her back and began wiping down the counters. With slumped shoulders and a heavy heart, Eliot started toward the kitchen.

A moment later, he stood at the end of the hall, grateful that Sophie was alone in the kitchen. His beautiful Sophie. Her back was to him as she swept up the floor. Carefully, slowly, he moved across the floor to her, and when he was only a few inches behind her she spun around.

Eliot knew that until the day he died, he would never forget the look of hate he saw reflected in her eyes. Eyes that normally only looked at him with love. He wanted to touch her, to try to explain. But that look said that he'd already been tried, found guilty and sentenced to a life without her love. But he couldn't give up that easily. Not after everything they'd come to mean to each other.

She placed the broom against a wall, walked right up to him, and Eliot held his breath, hoping, praying. Then she reached out and, with all the strength she could muster, slapped him hard across the face.

Chapter 24

"Baby, what can I say to you?" Eliot rubbed his stinging cheek, willing to take ten more blows if it would make her listen. "Tell me what I have to say to make this right."

Sophie stood glaring at him, the anger and hurt causing her whole body to tremble. The pure fury he saw in her eyes was unlike anything he'd ever imagined seeing there when she looked at him before. She loved him, or so she'd said. But that was yesterday, and it was a different man she loved. The man she thought he was.

"Tell me what to do. I can't lose you."

"Get out," she hissed between closed teeth.

"Sophie, please—"

"Get out! Get out of my store! Get out of my life! Get out!" She'd extended her arm toward the front hall, and even now Eliot could see the angry vibrations coursing through her slender frame.

What was left? He stood in place, hoping for some sudden inspiration. Some miracle. But none came. Finally, he turned and headed toward the front of the building.

At the entrance leading to the front of the store he stopped and turned. "I lied to you, and you will never have any idea how sorry I am for that. You can believe what you want; I know you will anyway. But what I feel for you, what we feel for each other, it's real, Sophie. As real as it will ever get. I love you, and I know you love me. Please, baby…please don't throw that away in anger."

He turned and headed out of the shop. He climbed into his car and pulled out of the parking lot. He headed toward Memphis with murder on his mind. Uncle Carl had been meddling in his life from the moment he had come to live with him. But this time the old man had gone too far. This time, he would pay for his interference and for the look of pain and hurt in Sophie's eyes— oh, yes, he would pay for that, too.

His cell phone rung, and he clicked on the headset. "What?"

"Eliot, it's me, Steve."

"Not a good time, Steve."

Steve sighed heavily. "I'm too late."

"Too late for what?"

"I wanted to warn you about Carl."

"Then, yeah, you're too late."

"Eliot, I know I shouldn't be telling you this, but the old man plans to cut you out of his will."

"Carl Fulton's fortune is the least of my concerns right now. I swear, Steve, I want to kill that son of a bitch."

"No, my friend, you don't kill men like Carlton with guns and knives. You want to get him where it hurts, in the wallet," the lawyer said.

"Then find me a weapon, Steve. Because one way or another, he's done." With that he turned off the phone and concentrated on driving. His mind drifted back to that morning. Waking up with Sophie curled against his side. The idea of never experiencing that again was unbearable.

All his adult life, Eliot thought he'd pushed down and conquered that lonely little boy he'd been when he arrived on his uncle's doorstep. But working at Mayfield had brought it all back. The feeling of family, the sense of belonging, the want, the need. They'd given him something he didn't even realize he was missing.

There was no way he could go back to the cold, empty existence he'd known before. That place was for the dead, and Sophie had brought him to life. She'd pumped her lifeblood into his heart. She was a permanent part of him now, nothing else would be acceptable.

Carl stood staring out the window of his office suite, and he felt the air shift around him. Eliot was coming.

Now that he'd cooled off, Carl could not understand what had possessed him to do what he did. It was like a compulsion. All he could think about was Eliot choosing his competition over him. It was betrayal. But now, considering the wheels he'd put in motion, he realized he'd overreacted. The problem with *over*-reactions was that you couldn't undo them. He'd put his nephew, his heir, in a position where he had to chose between him and the woman he loved.

He ran his hand over his face, suddenly feeling every one of his sixty-four years. Despite all his bluster, he knew there was no way he could cut Eliot out of his fortune. He'd nurtured and cultivated the boy all his life to take over the reins of Fulton Foods, and until recently Carl had been certain it had been the right decision. Eliot had shown himself worthy of his legacy in every way. But then again, Carl had never seen his nephew in love, and he knew from personal experience that that could change everything.

He listened as his door opened softly, but he never turned from the window. He'd expected a hurricane to come rushing through the office, but what had shown up instead was a quiet storm. Those were often the deadliest, he thought.

He took a deep breath and tried to defend himself. "I did it for your own good."

"As if you give a damn about anyone's needs but your own."

Slowly Carl turned to face his nephew and was startled by the broken man who stood in the doorway. "Your place is here."

Eliot laughed. Not a forced chuckle, but a pure, deep-throated laugh, and Carl began to wonder as to his mental state.

"You're kidding, right?" he finally managed to say through the laughter. "When has my place ever been here? You spent the majority of my youth making sure I understood that I was only *here* at your discretion. All my life, you've made me feel like a charity case, and that I owed you." The laughter had stopped, and now Eliot's voice had hardened. "And I paid you back, old man— I paid you back in sweat and tears! So don't you dare stand there and try to make me believe I ever had a place here."

Carl folded his arms across his chest and glared at his nephew. "Well, I can see there can be no reasoning with you," he said as he watched his nephew shake his head in dismay, and turn away with slumped shoulders. Then Eliot headed back out of the office, but he paused.

"You know…I had every intention of killing you, you evil-hearted monster. But the more I think about it, the more I realize living with yourself may be punishment enough." He started to walk away.

"Eliot!" Carl called out, and Eliot stopped. "What do you plan to do?"

Eliot glanced back over his shoulder and Carl saw the first sign of fire in his eyes. "I'm going to do what you trained me to do, Uncle Carl. I'm going to destroy my competition." With that he turned and walked out of Fulton Foods for the last time.

Three hours after Eliot had left the store, Sophie was working on the computer, looking over the books and trying to find a way to salvage the business. Mae came into the room with a sandwich plate and a can of soda pop. "I fixed you a sandwich," the older woman said.

"Thanks, Grandma, but I'm not hungry." Sophie shifted toward the computer screen so her grandmother couldn't see her red, swollen eyes.

"You haven't eaten all day. You're gonna make yourself sick."

"Really, I'm okay," she said, and continued reviewing the ledger.

"Sophie…" Mae pulled up a chair and sat beside her granddaughter. "Sophie, look at me."

Sophie quickly wiped at her eyes. "I'd rather not, Grandma."

Using her sternest voice, Mae sat up straight. "That wasn't a request, young lady."

Slowly, Sophie shifted in her seat to face her grandmother, and felt even worse as Mae's stern expression crumpled.

"Oh, my little baby." Sophie allowed herself to be pulled into the older woman's fragile arms. And as much as she tried to fight it back, the flow of tears went from a drizzle to a downpour of anguish.

"How could he do this to me?" she cried into her grandmother's shoulder, wrapping her arms around her waist. So many times she'd found comfort in these arms, but not this time. Nothing could comfort her this time.

"Shh, it's okay, little one." Mae stroked her hair, just as she'd done when she was a little girl. "It will be okay."

"No, it won't." Sophie sniffed loudly before pulling back out of Mac's warm arms. "I can't believe I was such an idiot. I fell for all his lies so easily. I never asked any questions." Reaching across the desk, she took a tissue from the box. "I had no business trying to go up against a big company like Fulton Foods. If I hadn't bid on their contracts, he would've never come here!"

Taking her face between her hands, Mae turned Sophie to face her. "Exactly. He would've never come here." Looking deep into her granddaughter's eyes, she asked, "Is that really what you would've wanted, Sophie—to never have met him?"

Sophie shook her head. "No. What I would've wanted was for him to be the arrogant, womanizing baker he was supposed to be."

"Oh, yes, I can see how that would've been an improvement," Mae said and laughed.

Sophie chuckled, realizing how ridiculous she sounded. But it was the truth. Because if he'd been that person, she could've forgiven him. But there was no way she could forgive him for this. There was no way they could go on from here. He'd allowed his uncle to sever the bridge tying them together, and that was what made her most angry. That he'd given them no way to be together. She wiped at her watery eyes again.

Damn him!

Sighing loudly, she turned back to the computer. "Well, I've been looking at the books, and we are going to have to let Wayne and Dante go," she said sadly. She swallowed over the lump in her chest, and continued. "Lonnie never really collected a salary, so she can just continue as she has been." She scrolled down the page. "We can get rid of the delivery van, and sell some of the new equipment. That should be enough to hold—"

"I'll work for free." Wayne spoke from the doorway.

Sophie jumped, startled to see him there. "Wayne, I couldn't ask you to do that."

"You didn't ask me."

"But you have bills to pay just like the rest of us."

He nodded. "I'll survive."

Sophie's eyes narrowed on his face, as a troubling thought passed through her mind.

"Not like that!" he snapped, as if reading her thoughts. "I have some money put away. It will hold me over until we get back up on our feet."

Sophie twisted her lips. "And what if we never get back up on our feet?"

He shrugged it off. "Then we don't. Either way, I'm here till the end."

Sophie glanced at her grandmother, remembering what she'd been told. "Grandma, can you give us a few minutes alone."

Mae nodded and stood. As she passed Wayne in the doorway, she reached out and squeezed his arm gently. He covered her hand, smiling down into her eyes.

Sophie knew that when the word *family* was used, most people automatically thought of blood relations. But she knew that a family could also be formed through common experiences and shared hardships. They were a family: a mentally challenged girl and the boy who loved her, an ex-con with a heart of gold, an elderly woman with a spine of pure steel and her. In all the ways that mattered, they were a family. And for a time, a sexy baker with secret, malicious intentions was also a part of that family.

But, try as she might, Sophie knew that was not all there was to Eliot. It was true she was instantly charmed by his handsome face and easy demeanor. But deep inside, she knew her heart was not so big a fool it would've made that enough. No, there was depth and soul to him. When he held her in his arms, when he spoke of his life with his parents and his dreams for his future, when he made love to her, the truth of him was revealed in those moments. And even now, her whole being craved that part of him, and would forever.

As Mae walked out of the office, Wayne closed the door behind her, and leaned his back against it. "Say it."

Sophie was startled by the bluntness in his voice, he was obviously expecting something. "Say what?"

"Say that you don't love me." He gestured to the tiny office. "That is why you needed this moment alone with me, right? To clear up any misconceptions I may have about your feelings for me?"

Okay, she thought, that's spooky intuitive. "Wayne, I do love you, but I'm not in love with you."

"I know that, Sophie. I'm not staying because I think something is going to happen between us," he said and he huffed loudly. "Look at you. In here crying your heart out over that jackass. How the hell could any man expect you to—" He shook his head. "Look, I'm not much for bullshit and you know it. So, I'm just going to say it like it is." He stood straight. "He doesn't deserve you. Not even. But for whatever reason, you love him, and I think you loved him almost instantly. From the day you came home from the hospital you took one look at him and I felt my heart break. Because in all the years I've known you, you never once looked at me like that. But it's cool." He sighed in resignation. "I let go of that dream a long time ago."

She stood to face him. "They why are you staying?"

"Because I owe you. You took a chance on me when no one else would. And never once did you or Mama Mae make me feel like an ex-con. Out there—" he gestured toward the wall "—my past is with me every day." He lifted his arms, revealing the prison tats that lined both forearms. "Anyone who recognizes these knows where I came from, and they treat me like I still belong there. You don't."

He moved across the room until he was standing directly in front of her. "When I walk in that front door every morning, I feel like a man. Just a man coming to do a job. You can't know how good that feels."

"But I can't afford to pay you."

He smiled, and with a quick movement pulled her against him and pressed his lips to her cheek. He was right, she realized. Whether Eliot had shown up or not, she would've never felt anything but friendship for Wayne.

With a final hug, he stepped back, a soft grin on his lips. "I knew you would feel good in my arms." He shook his head and turned toward the door. "Consider me paid in full," he called over his shoulder as he left the office.

Sophie leaned back against the desk and released a breath. A small part of her regretting the fact that her heart had not chosen Wayne.

Chapter 25

It was almost a week later. Sophie was alone in the office when the fax machine buzzed into life. She glanced at the machine, assuming it was another ad for diet pills, and turned back to the computer.

Something told her to check it out, so she snatched up the page and quickly read it. Her eyes widened and she sprung to her feet. She quickly reread the page and rushed into the kitchen where Wayne was cleaning an oven.

"It's an order!" She shook the page at him, before charging to the front of the store. "Grandma, it's an order! A new order!"

Mae was busy wiping down the front counters. She jumped in surprise as Sophie swept her up in a hug. "We got a new order! A big one!"

By that time, Wayne had joined her. "What are you talking about?" He grabbed the paper from her hand and read it. "Whoa, the city of Jackson!"

Unable to control her enthusiasm, Sophie hugged him, too. "Jackson Municipal Services! For a city of what? Fifty thousand?"

Mae clapped excitedly. "Oh, thank you, Jesus!"

"Probably more than that," Wayne said, frowning at the page. "Sophie, where did this come from?"

"It just came over the fax a few minutes ago."

"Did you submit a bid to them?"

She shook her head, as the euphoria began to slip away and Wayne's questions were ringing in her head. "No—I didn't. So how do they even know about us?" She reached for the fax.

"Exactly," Wayne answered, as he handed it over. "Why are they sending an order now? After everything that's happened?"

She reread the fax once more, this time very slowly, looking for any hidden clues as to the origins of the request. "I don't know," she muttered, then glanced up at both her grandmother and Wayne. "I plan to find out, but I'm also not going to look this gift horse in the mouth." She pointed to the page. "It says here they need the first delivery by Friday morning, so start measuring." She turned and headed back to the office. "I'm going to check this out."

But as she reentered the office, she stopped dead in her tracks because several pieces of paper lay on the floor and every few seconds more were pouring out of the machine. "Grandma! Wayne!"

Sophie began picking up the pages, glancing at them, trying to read as fast as they were coming. Each was a new order, some from large municipalities in the surrounding area, some from small businesses and organizations. Many of the businesses she had never heard of.

Wayne was also reading through the faxes. "What the hell is going on?" he asked in amazement. "I thought we were finished."

"So, did I," Sophie laughed, trying to organize the orders by requested delivery dates. "But, it looks like we're back in business."

Seeing the fat little stack of papers, Mae clapped her hands together. "Hot damn! I'm going to get my apron on." She hurried back to the kitchen, leaving a shocked Sophie and Wayne behind her.

"Did she just say *hot damn?*" Sophie asked. Her eyes twinkled with delight; she had never before heard her grandmother curse.

Wayne laughed. "That's what I heard."

"I think she's been spending too much time with you." Sophie laughed, too, feeling better than she had in over a week.

"Wayne!" Mae called from the kitchen. "I'm going to need some more bags of flour!"

Wayne shook his head at the summons. "I better hurry up before she tries to get it herself." He turned and headed out of the office, but stopped. "Hey, girl, don't know what you did, but way to go."

Alone in the office, Sophie continued sorting through the pages. She wasn't sure what she'd done, either, if anything. Something had changed in the past week. Maybe Fulton had decided to back off their lawsuit. She doubted it. That man had wanted blood. You don't give up a vendetta like that.

Sophie began calling the different companies to confirm the orders, and it didn't take her long to figure it out. The first couple of calls were awkward, as she didn't really know how to introduce herself. But soon, she was finding the code words to get the information she needed. Although the companies were in different cities and had different needs, they had all signed contracts Sophie had yet to see. And they had all dealt with her marketing director… Eliot Wright.

Sophie had never known exactly what Eliot did at his uncle's company. Only that he did it at Fulton Foods and he'd lied about everything. Apparently, he was some kind of marketing bigwig who could at once bolster his own interest while at the same time slicing and dicing the competition. And he was now using those skills in her interest—and against his uncle.

Sophie wondered if she should tell Mae and Wayne what she'd discovered. She finally decided not to. They needed this business too badly, and if they knew where it came from, pride might keep at least one of them from wanting to accept it.

But despite the fact that she could not reject his help, she needed him to understand it did not entitle him to anything. Digging around on the desk, she found the card Carl Fulton had basically thrown in her face a week ago.

She grabbed her purse and jacket and headed for the door. As she passed through the kitchen she called out, "I'll be back in a little while."

"You can't leave now!" Mae was standing with the walk-in refrigerator door open, about to go in. "We have all these orders to prepare."

"I know. I'll be back soon," she said, slipping her arms into her jacket.

"It's Eliot, isn't it? That's who did all this?"

Sophie glanced over her shoulder, searching for Wayne.

"He's out back in the shed getting flour. So tell me, am I right?"

"Yes." Her lips twisted in disdain. "Apparently, he's some kind of a marketing ace. That's what he did for his uncle."

Mae closed the fridge and walked toward her granddaughter. "Sophie, what are you about to do?"

"Talk to him." She glanced down at the floor. "Find out why. What does he expect."

"It's possible he's just trying to make up for what his uncle did."

"It's possible. I just want to make sure."

"Sophie, be careful. Sometimes we say things. Things we later wish we could take back. Right now, there's still something there between you two. Something that could probably be worked out in time."

"No there isn't."

"Don't go to him in anger and do something that can't be undone." Mae reached out and touched her arm. "Leave it alone for now. Just wait. When he's ready to explain he will. Just leave it be for now."

"I can't. I have to know what he expects."

Mae stood straight up, but even then she was a foot shorter than her granddaughter. The stern tone of her voice had returned. "I'll tell you what he expects. He expects you to forgive him eventually. And so do I."

Sophie's eyes widened in amazement. "Sorry, Grandma. If that's the case, you both will be disappointed."

Mae stared at her granddaughter for several long seconds, before finally shaking her head. "Not nearly as sorry as you will be if you cut ties with the man you love." She turned and went into the fridge.

Sophie sighed, feeling like the weight of the world was on her shoulders. She turned to leave and found Wayne standing in the back door with a bag of flour over his broad shoulder. She didn't know how much he'd overheard until she looked into his eyes and realized he'd heard just enough to hurt.

"Wayne, I—"

"We'll hold down the fort until you get back. Just hurry up." He carried the bag over to the mixer and pulling his small knife from his pocket began cutting the bag open.

An hour later she pulled into the driveway of the address on the card, and was surprised to find it was a high-rise condominium. As she pulled up to the valet attendant, she began having second thoughts. This was not where El would live. This concrete palace was nothing like him.

The attendant came forward with a smile to open her door, and she forced herself to step out. Slowly she approached the building, quickly scanning the card in her hand. Yes, this was the right address, but it just didn't feel right.

She went inside, got directions from the doorman and, taking the elevator, quickly reached the tenth floor. As the elevator doors closed behind her, she turned and stared at the gold-colored doors. Then the plush burgundy carpet that lined the hallway, the same as in the lobby. Tables bearing glass vases filled with fresh flowers lined the empty corridor.

Everything about the place screamed wealth, luxury and an elite lifestyle. And all she could think about was the down-to-earth workingman who'd flirted with her during his breaks. An image of him dressed in a sleeveless white T-shirt and loose jeans came to mind. She could just picture him with sweat causing the thin material to cling to his muscular chest. His back would be against the wall, one leg propped on a garbage can while he seduced her with his beautiful smile. God, how she missed that man.

At the end of the hall, a door opened and Eliot stepped out. At first he did not see her. He was locking his door and preparing to leave. He turned to head down the hall and stopped.

Sophie was so surprised to see him suddenly appear before her, she froze. They stared at each other, each surprised to see the other.

Slowly, he started down the hallway toward her. "Sophie?" He picked up his pace until he was almost running.

Realizing his intentions, she quickly put her hands out in front of her to block him. "Don't touch me!"

He stopped a few inches from her. His eyes narrowing in anger. "What?"

"I said don't touch me."

"Then why are you here?"

"To ask you why you sent us new clients."

His shoulders slumped and she suddenly understood why he thought she was there. It was just what she suspected. "Did you think you could buy me back?"

"Don't be stupid."

Sophie felt a sharp surge of anger. He looked so perfectly polished and aristocratic, and yet it was her El's voice and words coming from his mouth. "Go to hell!"

"You've already sent me there, baby."

She frowned, wanting to tell him that if that were the case then they were sharing the place. Instead, she said, "Just answer one question, and then I will leave and we will never have to see each other again."

He laughed. "Now, why would I find that the least bit appealing?"

"What?"

"You offer up the opportunity to never see you again like some kind of prize. Like it's something I want."

"Well, it's what *I* want."

His jawbone flexed with suppressed emotion, but in an even tone he said, "Then ask your question so we can both get on with our lives."

"What do I owe you for doing this?"

He tilted one of those arrogant eyebrows at her, and she felt herself melting inside. Why did this stranger have to look, act and sound so much like the man she wanted? Dressed in his expensive suit and loafers, he looked like a million bucks. She didn't know this man. So, why did he feel so familiar? So much like home?

"Hmm…" He rubbed his chin thoughtfully. "I hadn't thought about a price for my service." He grinned wickedly, as his amber eyes slid over her form. "But, since you're so willing to pay, why not?"

"You're such an arrogant jackass!"

"Maybe. Now…about that price."

"I knew you were no good, but thanks for reminding me."

He continued as if he had not heard her. "Oh, I know. How about a massage—in my hot tub?" He shrugged. "Of course, I'll leave the specifics up to you."

She shook her head. "I shouldn't have come here."

They looked at each other for several long seconds. "No, you shouldn't have," he finally said.

"I just wanted to tell you that anything you've done to help us is appreciated, but that's all, El…iot." She forced the unfamiliar name from her lips. Trying to make him an unknown entity and not the lover she thought she knew well. "A hearty thank-you is all it will get you. So, if you're helping us because you think you'll get me back, it won't work."

"Okay."

She stood stunned. She blinked trying to process the one word answer. *Okay?*

With a jerky nod of her head, she turned to the elevator and pushed the button. "Well…goodbye, Eliot, and again, thank you for all your help."

"Uh-huh." He stood beside her and stared at the numbers overhead.

What the hell? One minute he's acting like he can't live without me and in the next like he doesn't even know me?!

She glanced at him as he pulled out his cell phone to make a call.

Feeling like something had just reached inside and ripped out her heart, she glanced down at the purse in her hands. She looked at the flowers on a nearby table. Half-listening as he discussed business on the phone, she checked out her cuticles and decided to get a manicure soon. She looked anywhere but at him.

He'd been the greatest love of her life, the man of her dreams, the one she would remember for the rest of her life and the final word of the relationship had been *uh-huh*.

Finally, the elevator doors opened and revealed an empty car. She walked in, followed closely by Eliot. She tried fighting back the tears in her eyes, not sure what was worse: knowing she'd been duped, or knowing she'd meant so little to him.

Unable to stop the tears from flowing, she quickly looked down at the floor. She wanted to wipe them away, but he would see. This was pathetic. Here she was so confused and strung out on him that she was about to have a nervous breakdown, and he was satisfied with *uh-huh*.

Suddenly the car came to a screeching halt and Sophie found herself thrown against the wall.

Chapter 26

She looked up to see Eliot standing beside the controls, as calm as a summer day. *Had he pushed the button on purpose?*

"What are you doing?" She finally wiped at her eyes, having a hard time seeing through the tears.

"Finally…" He released a heavy sigh. "I was starting to think you were made of stone."

"What are you talking about?"

He walked to her, and lifting a finger he caught a tear on his hand. "This is real. Not all that bluster and bullshit you were giving me in the hall. *This.*" He lifted his hand to show her the tiny puddle of water in his palm. "*This* I believe."

She concentrated as hard as possible but was unable to stop the flow of tears. "I hate you," she finally cried out. "I hate you so much!"

"No, baby…you hate that you *can't* hate me. You want to." He huffed. "I know, because I want to hate you, too."

"Start this elevator car, right now!"

"No, not until we get some things straightened out."

"Start this car, El! I mean it!"

"We need to talk, really talk, and this is the only place we can."

"The alarm will go off soon, then what will you do?" She smirked.

"Not unless someone attempts to open the door." His eyes narrowed. "And don't even think about it."

"Fine! You want to talk? Talk!" She folded her arms across her chest and backed into the corner.

"I swear." He shook his head. "It's like trying to hug a cactus."

She huffed. "Well, *this cactus* doesn't want your hugs."

He moved closer. "*This cactus* needs hugs more than most." Bracing an arm on either side of her head, he effectively locked her in place. "What's changed, Sophie? Can you tell me that? You're still the woman you were last week. I'm still the same man—"

"No! You're not!"

"Do I sound any different? Do I look any different?" Lifting her hand, he pressed it against his chest, and she tried to ignore the rapidly beating heart beneath the suit jacket. "Do I feel any different?"

"Define *different*."

"What?"

"Define *different*. Elberto, the man you pretended to be—is he real and therefore *different* from Eliot, the heir to the Fulton fortune? Which is real, Eliot or Elberto? How would I know different, if I don't know the real you?"

"You know the real me."

"Everything you told me was a lie."

"Not everything."

"Everything!"

"Come on, Sophie, you know that's not true."

"You have got my head so screwed up, I have no idea what is true! Is the man I fell in love with true or just a figment of my imagination? How can I ever be sure?"

"You're just going to have to trust me."

She laughed. "Plleeaasse."

Eliot stared at her.

"You're kidding me! Everything you told me from the moment we met was a lie. And I'm supposed to just *trust* you? How many kinds of fool do you think you can make me?"

"You're not a fool. Just a little too trusting."

"Not anymore. Thank you for the education." She was having a hard time ignoring his familiar musk cologne. It was working on her sense like an aphrodisiac.

He was watching her carefully, as if he were trying to see inside her head. She looked away, and he tilted his head to maintain eye contact.

"Sophie, have I ever told you how your eyes sparkle when you're thinking about sex?" He smiled. "It was the main reason I couldn't resist you—I *did* try. But then you would look at me with those hungry eyes." He took a deep breath. "Those sweet, hungry eyes. What man could walk away from that? Your eyes would sparkle the way they're sparkling now," he said. He leaned even closer until his hot breath was on her neck.

Sophie swallowed, feeling his lips so close to the skin of her neck. So close. "Leave me alone," she whispered.

"I can't."

"I don't want to have sex with you."

"Yes, you do."

"I despise you."

"Maybe, but that doesn't change what we both want."

"I don't want you."

His eyes dropped to his chest, then back up to hers. "Look."

Sophie followed his eyes and realized at some point she'd reached up and taken hold of his jacket lapels. She instantly released him, and the shock did what anger could not. It stopped the tears.

"Do you really want to ruin both our lives over one idiotic move?"

Sophie couldn't answer. She was too shaken up by her body's involuntary reaction to him.

"Close your eyes."

"No."

He tilted his head to the side. "I promise not to kiss you, just close your eyes."

"No."

"Okay. I was on my way out to find you some more clients, but if you'd rather spend the day trapped in an elevator with me, I'm willing to accommodate you," he said.

"Fine." She closed her eyes and then they instantly popped back open. "But I swear, you better not try anything." Then she closed her eyes once again.

"Now, try to imagine yourself in ten years. Imagine what you would look like, how you may have changed, and the goals you've set for yourself."

"Why?"

"Just do it."

She released a heavy sigh. "This is silly."

"Tick, tock, tick—"

"Fine, I see myself in ten years."

"Where are you?"

"Why does that matter?"

"Where are you?"

Another deep sigh. "I'm in the bakery. Grandma has retired, so I'm running the store."

"Who's there besides you…and Wayne."

She smiled. "What makes you so sure Wayne will be there?"

"Trust me, Wayne's there. Who else?"

"Lonnie and Dante, and the *real* baker I hired ten years before to replace you. He's wonderful by the way, in the bakery *and* in the bedroom."

El smiled at the smug little smirk on her lips. "I can't believe this. You're actually trying to make me jealous of a figment of your imagination."

"Let's not forget *you're* a figment of the imagination."

"No baby, I'm a real, flesh-and-blood man, no matter how you may want to deny it."

"Eliot Wright is real, El was a dream—or should I say nightmare."

"We're getting off track. Who else is in the bakery with you?"

"I've had to hire all kinds of new staff to service our huge and growing clientele." She smiled, truly seeing that future now and liking what she was seeing. "We gained many more clients after Fulton Foods went out of business," she said sarcastically.

"You won't have to wait long for that," he muttered.

Her eyes popped open. "What do you mean?"

"Don't worry about it. Close your eyes."

"El, don't try to take on your uncle—"

"Close your eyes, stubborn woman."

Hesitantly, she closed them again.

"Who else is there, other than the staff?"

She frowned. "Who else would be there?"

"A husband, maybe a child or two. Who do you share your life with, Sophie?"

"I don't know. I'm still getting over you."

"But you can see someone in your future?"

"I don't know. Maybe."

He watched the pained expression cross her face.

"Where am I?"

"How would I know?"

"Aren't we still in touch?"

"Of course not!"

"Why not?"

Her eyes popped open. "Because ten years ago you broke my heart and made it impossible for me to ever love another man as much as I loved you."

El looked directly into her eyes. "Do you ever think about me?"

Sophie hesitated for several long seconds before saying, "All the time."

"Why don't you pick up the phone and call me?"

"Because it still hurts."

"But not as much as it used to?"

She looked away. "No, not as much. Besides, you probably already married."

"No, I never did."

"Really?" She looked into his eyes.

"Really. I spent the years trying to find a woman to fill the void you left in my life, but it was never right. And I couldn't bring myself to settle for less than what we had. But I do still think about you all the time, and occasionally I drop by and visit Mama Mae and she keeps me up to date on how your life is going."

"You'd actually try to pump information out of my grand-mother?"

"I wouldn't have to try; she would willingly offer it. She still loves me, unlike her granddaughter. She always wished we could've worked things out."

Sophie felt an eerie chill run down her spine, remembering Mae's parting words as she left the bakery earlier.

As if he'd worked some kind of magic spell on her, Sophie was amazed to find the pain of his betrayal did seem less sharp than earlier that morning. It was as if he'd really transported them through time and allowed her to see that the pain would eventually heal.

She pushed against him, and moved away from the corner. "This is silly."

"I agree. Two people, both miserably unhappy for the rest of their lives, all because of one really stupid mistake that will one day be long forgotten. You're right, that is silly." He came up behind her. "Can't you see it, Sophie? A future where you and I are running the bakery together? Our children eventually getting big enough to help out, and then we'll teach them the business so they can pass it on to the next generation. All our days together, all our nights together." He slipped his arm around her waist. "Can't you see it, Sophie?"

Feeling weak with need, she laid her head back against his chest. "Don't do this to me, El."

"I've gotten a little gray around the edges, thanks in part to that stubborn-as-a-mule daughter you gave me." He laid a pos-sessive hand across her midsection. "And your perfect flat stomach now has a few beautiful stretch marks." He kissed her cheek. "I like to think of them as battle scars."

"Please, El, I'm not this strong."

"We have a beautiful home now, and the mortgage to go with it, but we still keep the little room in the back of the bakery for our afternoon rendezvous. One day our youngest son found it and asked why we kept a bed in there. Remember the lame excuse you gave him?"

She shook her head, refusing to get caught in the wonderful imaginary future he was painting right before her eyes.

"Sure you do," he continued. "You told him that we kept it there in case one of the customers fainted while in the store."

She glanced over her shoulder. "That's the best you could do? You're right, that is lame."

"Don't blame me. It was *your* explanation."

"I'd come up with something a lot more clever than that."

"Oh, really?"

"Yes, for instance, I'd tell him we kept it in there as a memorial of when we first met. He'd of course ask what I meant, and I'd tell him the story of how I came home from the hospital on crutches and there you were."

"And I'd tell him how the first time I laid eyes on you I knew I had to have you."

"And I'd tell him what a filthy, lying bastard you were, and how all the time you were plotting and conniving to run us out of business."

He kissed her cheek again. "And I'll tell him how you punished me for that, by scaring me to thinking we would never be together again. And then how you forgave and redeemed me and made me a better man."

She stepped out of his arms and turned to face him. "If you want redemption, talk to God."

"I just want you, and that future I can see so clearly." He held out his hand to her. "Well…what will it be, Sophie? Are we going up or down?"

"Neither." She wrapped her arms around his neck, pressing her lips to his, and Eliot eagerly accepted the invitation. Lifting her from beneath each thigh, he wrapped her slender legs around his waist and backed her against the wall.

Chapter 27

Feeling his body pressed to hers, Sophie wanted to shout her joy and satisfaction to the heavens! How she'd missed this. The feel of his large hands holding her thighs in his firm grip as his mouth took hers.

"I promise, Sophie, no more secrets," he said. Pressing his groin against her center, he simulated all the things he would do to her. And as always, it felt like he was issuing a silent challenge. Daring her to meet his passion with hers. And when she tried, he'd only push her further and further until Sophie was certain there could be nowhere else left to go.

"I've missed you," he said, and then moaned against her shoulder. "Don't ever push me out again. Please, baby, hit me, throw something at me if you have to, but being away from you is torture I cannot stand."

Sophie had no words for him. All she could do was tell him with her body what she wanted. She wrapped her arms around his waist, her fingers wiggling beneath the material of his jacket, and he instantly understood. They pulled the jacket off his shoulder and threw it across the car.

She began to unbutton his dress shirt, and he quickly took over, so she turned her attention to his tie. Soon his beautiful, muscular chest was revealed. The soft, brown curls that sprinkled it led down into his slacks.

Sophie ran her fingers down that line, thinking that had to be one of the sexiest parts of a man's body. The way their chest hair served as a treasure map. She quickly pulled her shirt over her head, and he came to her at once. Pulling the white bra straps down her arms, baring her shoulders for his mouth.

She went weak-kneed as his open mouth clamped down on a shoulder. His large hands wrapped around her bottom, pulling her up against his hard arousal. There were always too many clothes between them.

Feeling his throbbing organ pushing into the crotch of her jeans, Sophie opened her legs wider. He took the invitation and pushed hard against her, rubbing deep into her slit. The tough blue jeans didn't stand a chance against a man determined to reach his destination.

The bra slipped off a breast as his hungry mouth took its place, sucking her into the warm cavity. His tongue circled and darted around the hardened nipple until it was sore with his attention. As if sensing her growing discomfort, he released the other and turned his attention there.

"El." Her head moved left and right, seeking, wanting, not knowing how to tell him. Her mind was scrambled with the sensory delights coming at her from all angles. All she could do was stand pressed against the wall where he held her, accepting and waiting for whatever would come next.

She didn't have to wait long. He moved like a bolt of lightning. Kneeling before her, he quickly unsnapped her jeans and pulled them down over her hips.

Plunging his tongue in the V-crotch of her silky panties, he licked and laved until they were wet with both his juices and hers. She twisted restlessly, wanting the jeans off, wanting his mouth fully against her.

But still he continued to torment her. His hands, wrapped around her bare bottom, squeezed the pliable flesh between his fingers. Firmly holding a cheek in each hand so she could not squirm out of his reach.

Feeling the fire at the core of her being beginning to burn out of control, Sophie grabbed on to his soft locks, trying to find some stabilizing force as the first wave washed over her. Her whole body trembled in release, and before the sensations had even stopped, he was pulling her jeans down farther. Lifting first one leg, then the other, he peeled away her tennis shoes and pants and tossed them aside.

Sophie thought how awkward she must look, standing there completely bare except for her bra, which was still snapped around her midsection. Eliot couldn't have cared less as he stood before her, unbuttoning his pants.

He gave them one hard push to get them down around his hips. From a pocket he produced a condom and quickly slipped it over the head of his full erection, then lifted her again. Looking directly into her eyes, he pushed her against the wall once more, but this time it was with him buried deep inside her.

Eliot held her firmly in place. As he pushed even deeper inside her, he whispered in her ear, "Open for me, baby."

And she tried, using his shoulders to pull herself up. She cried out as she felt him sinking even farther into her center. She felt her body stretching to accommodate him as he continued to go even deeper.

"El, I can't…" she moaned, far beyond the ability to form complete sentences. With her face pressed against his bare chest, she could hear his pounding heart racing beneath his skin.

"Ssh, yes, you can," he said quietly, his deep voice rumbling from somewhere over her head, his throbbing organ growing inside her.

"El—I…" She shook with force, crying out, her back arching as the second orgasm struck her with an unexpected suddenness.

Eliot held her tightly in his arms as he was drenched in liquid woman. "That's it, baby, that's it," he said between gritted teeth, as his orgasm followed on the end of hers.

His arms tightened around her body as he pushed one of her legs farther up on his hip, opening her wider. Taking long strokes, he rode his release to completion, pushing relentlessly into her body until Sophie didn't think she could take any more.

Then suddenly another orgasm followed his, and she gripped his strong arms and rode the wave. As she slowly came down from the final orgasm, she laid her head on his broad shoulder. Feeling wonderfully exhausted, she opened her eyes and found herself looking directly at a small, black bulb in the far top corner of the elevator.

"El?"

"Hmm?" he muttered, placing gentle kisses along her shoulder and arm.

"Is that a camera?"

He froze, then slowly turned to look over his shoulder. "Oh shit!"

Like cold water being poured over their heads, the sensual mood evaporated as he dropped her legs. He scrambled around to get her clothes and pushed them into her hands. Lifting his arms, he tried to block her from the camera. "Hurry up, and get dressed," he said.

She quickly shimmied into her jeans and briefly glimpsed a serious frown on his face. Then pushed her bra back in place up on her shoulders, and he watched with growing desire as she recupped her breasts. By the time she slipped her top over her head, Sophie was shivering with pent-up laughter.

Soon, El was laughing with her. He rested his forehead on her shoulder, and sighed. "I bet I know what we'll be discussing at the next tenant meeting." And then they both burst into laughter again.

Later that night, their bodies twined together in his large bed, Eliot held her arms over her head as he entered her body once again. The moonlight streaming through the slightly opened window brought with it a cool late summer breeze.

"I love you, Sophie," he whispered against her hair. He knew that no place in the world could ever feel as good or right as where he was right now. Buried deep inside this woman he adored.

"I love you, too," she moaned, her back arching as she welcomed him into her.

Shifting his body weight to his elbows, he put his lower back to work, slowly thrusting and withdrawing from her, until she was clinching to hold him inside. Still he continued his slow assault, pausing occasionally to hold back the quickly rushing orgasm. He wanted this to last as long as possible.

He leaned back on one elbow, cupping a small, perfectly formed breast in his hand. He simply held it, enjoying the play of the moonlight across her flawless, dark skin.

"What?" she asked, seeing his thoughtful expression.

"You're so beautiful."

"According to you."

He shifted back over the top of her. "Does anyone else's opinion matter?"

She smiled. "No."

"Then my assessment stands. You're beautiful."

Her smiled widened. "As long as you think so, I'm a happy woman."

Pulling back, he watched the emotions run across her face, as he pushed into her…pleasure. As he pulled back…regret, and then he returned, plunging deep inside…relief.

She was indeed beautiful, everything from the softly perfect body that brought him hours and hours of pleasure to her kind heart and generous nature. He loved that she was sharp-minded and could match wits with him on almost any topic, but she wasn't showy about her intellect. Never needing to prove anything to anyone. She was comfortable in her skin and confident in her ability. Eliot knew that they were the perfect complements to each other.

She pushed herself on him, trying to force him to move. But Eliot only grinned wickedly down at her face. "No, you made me wait too long for this. I plan to enjoy every minute of it."

"What about me?" She pouted coyly. "I need you right now."

He chuckled and winked. "We'll take care of you next time."

She punched his arm. "Oh, no, you didn't just say that!"

He laughed, and released an exaggerated sigh. Then quick as a flash, he moved, lifting both her legs over his shoulder, leaving her wide open as he drove himself to her very center.

"Is that better?" He gritted his teeth, fighting to hold back his release once again. She felt so damn good, it was incredible that he'd held off this long.

"Yes, oh, yes, much better," she whined. Reaching up, she grabbed the headboard. "Love me, El, please…please!"

If there was a man out there somewhere strong enough to resist such a plea, Eliot knew he'd never met him. And he certainly was not that man. Bracing his body on his hands, he lifted himself and sunk deep inside her.

A deep growl escaped his throat as she exploded around him. Bucking beneath him, she whimpered and moaned as the ecstasy of the moment washed over her.

Eliot was closely following, but he fought with everything in him, needing to be with her like this as long as possible. Sweat was rolling in streamlets down the center of his back to his narrow waist, and then her hands were there. Around his waist holding him, while she pushed herself on him, gyrating against him, and finally he could not hold back any longer as he poured his soul into her.

Chapter 28

Sometime in the night, El reached out his arm looking to sweep Sophie against his side, but she wasn't there. Panicked, he sat up in the bed and breathed again when he saw her clothes still thrown across a nearby chair.

He glanced around but did not see her. Climbing out of bed, he wandered into the living room, and there she was. Even in the dark he could make out her slender form. She was standing in front of his bookcase, which took up one wall of the room.

"You okay?" he asked, rubbing at his blurry eyes.

"Yes," she said, but her voice sounded strained.

"What's wrong?" Still half-asleep, he padded across the room to her.

She turned to him, her arms stretched out to encompass the whole area. "Is this who you are? Really who you are?"

He paused. They'd spent the night making love, but the problems of the day before still hung in the air between them. "Yes," he said.

She smirked, slightly angry at his blunt answer. He wondered if he should've lied to spare her feelings.

No, that's how I got in this mess to begin with.

She turned back and continued looking at books, and Eliot crossed the room to turn on the lights.

He could see she was dressed in his robe, which looked adorably oversized, seductively hanging off one shoulder. "What'd you do that for?" she snapped, covering her burning eyes.

"Consider it a metaphor," he snapped back. He'd had enough apologizing and begging. He wanted them to be done with this so they could get on with their lives. He wanted to marry this woman and build that future he'd told her about earlier. And they would never do that if every time she saw something unfamiliar, something she didn't know about him, she started hating him all over again.

"I love books, so much so it's hard for me to give one up, so I ended up with this." He nodded toward the wall. "You like books, too."

"Doesn't make us soul mates," she muttered, determined to be disgruntled.

He walked over to the bookcase and, reaching overhead to a shelf of oversized books, he grabbed a thick one and brought it down.

"Here," he said, plopping it in her hands. He then crossed to the leather sofa and fell back on it.

"What's this?"

"My mother's recipe book." He yawned. "It's how I learned to bake."

She looked up at him, more interested than she wanted to admit. "Really?"

"Yep."

She sat down on the floor in front of the bookcase and started glancing through the pages. "These look like Grandma's recipes."

"They're not. I thought the same thing the first time I saw the book in the store. But after I compared the two books, I realized your grandmother's book has a lot of herbs and spice in the recipes. Things I never would've imagined in pastries. Not sure where she got them, but they are some of the best pastry recipes I've ever tasted." He smiled. "You know, that was the first thing that struck me about the place when I first arrived. How much

Mama Mae reminded me of my mother." He smiled. "That ol' school breed of mama—love you to death, but don't take any mess off you."

Sophie smiled. "That's her." She glanced at him. "Where's your mother?"

"She and my father died in a car accident when I was ten. That's how I ended up with Uncle Carl."

She frowned. "I'm surprised he was willing to take you in."

El huffed. "He was more than willing. My parents named my father's sister, my Aunt Carol, as my guardian. But Uncle Carl fought her for custody and won."

"How? I mean, your parents left a will, so it's not like there was any question of what they wanted, right?"

"He had better resources and more money to spend on lawyers." Eliot sighed. "In the end, he painted my Aunt Carol as unfit because she worked for a janitorial service and lived in a one-bedroom apartment. The court agreed I would be better off with him."

Sophie's frown deepened. "Why would he do that?"

El sat for a moment thinking of the past. He pondered the unusual hand fate had dealt him, and how all those things had brought him to this place in his life. For so many years, he'd hated the fact that he ended up in his uncle's custody, but had he not, he would have never met Sophie.

"When Carl took over the reins of Fulton Foods from his father, he let it consume his life. He's managed to build it to twice the size it was when his father died. But time got away from him. He never married, or had any children." Eliot looked directly at Sophie. "I am the only child of his only sibling. Apparently, when I was born he tried to talk my parents into letting me come live with him then, promising to make me his heir. They refused." El shrugged, fighting to hold back the bad memories. "And then they died."

"Wow." She tilted her head, watching him with a wary expression. "So, how was it? Growing up with your uncle?"

His lips twisted in a sarcastic expression. "You've met my uncle."

"Understood." She bit her lip, and he could see she was trying to find some good in the situation.

"Don't bother, Sophie. The man is rotten to the core. I spent the greater part of my youth trying to find the good in him. There is none." He laid his head back against the sofa. "He took me from my aunt to make me his heir, but every time I did something that displeased him, he'd try to use the threat of leaving me out of his will as a way to control me."

He laughed. "The funniest part is that I didn't care about his will, or his money or his company. I was so miserable without my parents that I didn't care about anything. Until…"

"Until?"

"Until I got old enough to understand how much *he* cared." His head came up and he looked at her with narrowed eyes. "Then I wanted it all. His fortune, his position, everything he cared about—I wanted to take it all from him," he said bitterly.

"No, El, don't." She shook her head emphatically. "Don't allow yourself to be consumed by that kind of hatred. You'll end up just like him."

He gave her a soft smile. "I'll have you to save me."

"I told you, redemption is God's business, not mine. I'm just a woman."

He got on his knees and began crawling across the floor to her. "But, oh, what a woman." He stopped in front of her, his face only inches from hers. "This conversation is depressing."

"Actually, it's pretty wonderful." She reached out and touched his face. "Everything you've said feels like the truth."

"It is. But it's still depressing." He moved forward, bearing her down to the carpeted floor and settling into the crook of her body. "I much prefer to do this."

"Surprise, surprise."

"So…? Are we okay?"

"Yes. But one day I want to hear the rest. I feel like you know so much about me and my world, and I've only had a glimpse of yours." She frowned, as if a sudden unpleasant thought occurred to her. "You were right, by the way—about Lonnie."

"Really?" He tried to hide a smile.

"Go ahead and laugh. That little hussy has been playing me for years. Here I'm living like a monk, and she's bonking like a sailor on shore leave."

This time he did laugh. "*That's* why you're mad? She was getting some and you weren't?"

"No, and I'm not mad. If I had been paying closer attention I would've realized she was growing up and changing. Anyway, I guess I'm grateful it was Dante, someone who really cares about her. Someone else could've really taken advantage of her."

"That's true."

"El? What did you mean in the elevator when you said I wouldn't have to wait long for Fulton to go out of business?"

Suddenly, he rolled off her and sat up. "Don't worry about it."

"Having met your uncle, it's kind of hard not to."

"Have a little faith in me."

"I have all the faith in the world in you, but I also know what a feud can do to a family."

"There is no feud."

"Really?"

"A feud is an ongoing disagreement." He glanced over his shoulder at her. "There is no feud."

"Then what are you doing?"

"Exacting vengeance."

"El—"

"Shh," he said, and turned on his side to lie beside her. "Don't worry about what is going on between me and my uncle. You just focus on the new clients I'm sending you, and taking care of your grandmother."

"I want a long, full life with you, Mr. Wright. Now that I've found you."

"And we will have that. I just have a little unfinished business, that's all."

She tilted her head to look at him. "Obviously, you're not going to give this up, and quite frankly, I'm too sleepy to care about it right now." She stood and stretched. "Come on, let's go back to bed."

He stood beside her and, taking her hand, headed toward the bedroom. She paused beside a statue of a phoenix, and he turned to see what had caught her attention.

"I like the symbolism of the phoenix." He answered the unasked question in her eyes.

She smiled. "You're kinda deep, huh?"

He arched an eyebrow. "Not yet, but come on into the bedroom and I'll rectify that."

She laughed. "I mean it. Here I thought you were this arrogant pastry chef and now…it's like I've all of a sudden started dating someone else, and I'm getting to know him for the first time." She reached up and placed a quick kiss on his lips before walking ahead to the bedroom.

He followed at a more sedate pace, deep in thought. "What if that's true?"

"What?" she asked, dropping the robe she was wearing. She began to crawl across the bed, and Eliot suddenly lost his train of thought.

Quickly he came up behind her. "Wait, don't move," he whispered, holding her by the hips, he held her in place on her knees. "Perfect," he purred, climbing onto the bed behind her. "Absolutely perfect." He ran a hand over her hip, and around her firm bottom.

"Don't move," he instructed once more, before reaching into the nightstand and quickly finding a condom. Looking back at her perfectly positioned on the bed, he hurried and donned the latex cover, then came up behind her once more.

"I've been dreaming about this position for weeks," he whispered in her ear, as he guided himself inside her. "Did you miss me? When we were apart?" he asked, before running his tongue over her earlobe.

"Uh-huh," she managed between stilted breaths, her focus split between what was going on behind her and what was going on inside her.

Holding her hips in place, El pulled back a fraction. "I don't believe you." He held himself at her wet opening, just waiting. "I'll ask again. Did you miss me?"

"Yes," she said, and moaned.

"Hmm." He pushed forward a fraction. "That sounded a little more believable."

"El!"

He laughed and moved a fraction deeper inside her. "Once again. Did you miss me?"

She pushed back, trying to bring him inside her. Her small elbows dug into the comforter as she grinded against him in frustration. "Yes, damn you! Yes!"

"That's what I'm talking about." He kissed her shoulder, even as he planted himself deep inside her body. Using all his skill as a lover, he wrapped himself around her body and pumped into her. He held back when he felt her reaching for the finish line, and when she began to cool, he held her hips and pushed her to the limit once more, until finally he could not hold her back any longer and she screamed his name as her release forced his. Together they leaped off the cliff and into the abyss.

An hour later, curled against his side, Sophie said, "You know when I drove up to this place today, I didn't think I had the right place. It's so different from where I imagined you would live." She glanced around the ultramodern bedroom, with its sharp angles and sleek lines, and nodded. "But now, I think it does kind of fit you—in a way."

"Think you can get used to the place?"

She looked up at his face. "What do you mean?"

"Living here."

"Here? In Memphis? I can't live this far from the bakery, what if something happens in the middle of the night?"

"What if…what if you moved the bakery here?"

"Why would I do that?"

He sighed, as if he were about to reveal something he didn't want to. "Make no mistake, Sophie. When all is said and done, I plan to put my uncle out of business. And there will be a huge opening here. An opening you will be perfectly posed to fill."

She sat up in the bed. "How long have you been working on this?"

He folded his arms behind his head. "Long enough to have most of the pieces in place. Any day now I expect Humpty Dumpty to take a tumble."

She huffed. "Problem is this particular Humpty Dumpty may get up and wipe the floor with you."

"Sophie, I know you've only seen one side of me, but I've spent my life learning at the foot of the master of deceit and double dealing. He wanted to make me ruthless, and to a point he succeeded. I'm better equipped than anyone for the task of bringing down Carl Fulton."

El blinked away the fierceness he was feeling, seeing the wary concern come into her eyes. No matter what she said, El realized she still saw her gentle pastry chef when she looked at him. And that was fine, because that was also a part of who he was.

But she'd yet to fully understand there was also another part of him. The side of him that wanted revenge for the lost little boy he'd once been. The part of him willing to do anything, cross any line and take on any man who threatened what he loved. Before he was finished with him, his uncle Carl would know that the student had finally surpassed the master.

Chapter 29

It happened sooner than even Eliot imagined. The next day he awoke to pounding on his front door. He scrambled from the bed, where Sophie still slept and gently pulled the bedroom door shut as he went to answer the door.

He looked through the peephole and considered not opening the door. But he knew his uncle would not go away that easily. He took a deep breath and opened it.

Carl stormed into the apartment. "You ungrateful bastard!" He began pacing across the room, and Eliot quickly realized his uncle was avoiding eye contact. "I took you into my home. I raised you like you were my own son. Made you a part of my business—in fact, I was planning to leave the whole thing to you, but there won't be anything to leave now! Are you trying to ruin me?"

Eliot sat down in a nearby chair. "Yes."

The answer so stunned Carl, he spun around to El and saw the truth reflected in his nephew's eyes. Carl's eyes widened and he temporarily stopped breathing. Then his coppery brown skin turned a deep shade of red. "You think you can ruin me?! Me?!

I saved your little narrow ass from a life of poverty with that toilet-cleaning aunt of yours! I made you a man! And you think *you* can ruin *me?!*"

Eliot smiled slowly, with as much malicious intent as he could muster. "You're here, aren't you?"

"You insolent little punk! Who do you think you are?"

Eliot's eyes narrowed. "I'm what you made me, Uncle Carl. I'm a businessman."

Carl stared at him for several seconds, before he finally nodded. "So you think you got me, huh?" Something in his eyes warned Eliot, and he decided not to answer.

Mentally, he ran through his checklist looking for a loop hole he might have missed in his planning. But he'd been meticulous. He'd managed to undercut Carl with over sixty percent of his clients, doing it in a way that did not breach any legal boundaries. Carl had taught him that there was a way around any law, and his job was to find all those ways. He had, and now Carl was feeling the result.

Carl reached into his jacket pocket and pulled out two folded sets of papers. He tossed both at Eliot, and turned toward the door to leave.

Eliot jumped off the couch as if Carl had just tossed a couple of snakes at him. "What's this?" He picked up first one then the other, not believing what he was seeing.

"One's your heart, and the other is your soul. You decide which you value more." With that Carl turned and walked out of the condo, slamming the door behind him.

Shortly after, Eliot heard the bedroom door starting to open. He quickly scooped up the papers and tucked them in his nearby desk drawer. He turned to the bedroom door just as it opened, and Sophie stepped out, wearing his robe once more.

He pasted on a smile. "Morning, gorgeous."

Sophie smiled, sleepily. "Morning, yourself." She nodded toward the door. "Who was that?"

"Uncle Carl—believe it or not."

"Come to beg your forgiveness and call it a truce?"

Eliot laughed. "Um, not quite." He started walking toward her. "Hungry?"

"Starving."

"Great. Let me shower and then I will make you a world-class breakfast."

"Sounds good to me. I'll start the coffee."

"See? I told you we make a great team. The kitchen is right through there." Eliot kissed her forehead, then headed toward the master bathroom.

Sophie quickly started the coffee, then hurried back into the living room. She waited until she heard the shower going, before slowly opening the desk drawer.

"I promise, Sophie, no more secrets," she muttered in a whiny voice, imitating what El had told her only the day before.

She'd been wakened by Carl's ranting and raving and had heard most of it. She'd also seen him toss the papers at El before leaving. She'd watched through a crack in the door as Eliot hid the papers from her. *No more secrets, huh?*

Sitting down on the couch, she quickly read through the papers, her eyes widening as she read both sets and compared the two.

One set was proprietary papers signing over Carl's controlling interest in Fulton Foods to Eliot, effective immediately. Eliot could be the CEO of Fulton Foods by the time he dressed and left for the office. The thing he most wanted, to strip Carl of all he held dear, was right there within his grasp.

But the second set of papers was the one that grabbed Sophie's attention. They were a set of documents canceling the legal proceedings. Halfway down the third page was a paragraph that was the crux of it. It stipulated that part of the agreement would be Eliot no longer acting on the behalf of Mayfield Bakery, surrendering his stock interest in Fulton Foods and resigning his position.

So the choices he'd been given were to stop the lawsuit, which meant he would have to abandon his plans to destroy his uncle's company. Or, he could completely turn his back on her and the bakery and inherit his uncle's empire, effectively destroying Carl with a single stroke of the pen.

With the two sets of papers, his uncle was asking one basic

question: Which was more important to Eliot? Helping her or destroying his uncle? And he'd framed both documents in a way that Eliot could not have both. He would have to choose. His heart or his soul.

As the shower stopped, Sophie quickly refolded the papers and put them back in the drawer. She understood now why Eliot had hid them. If he'd shown her the papers, then he would've felt obligated to save the bakery. Even if that was not the choice he would've wanted to make.

Sophie took her own quick shower, slipping back on the clothes she'd worn there. By the time she finished dressing, breakfast was ready. It was a quick and easy menu of scrambled eggs, several strips of perfectly crisp bacon, a half-dozen cinnamon rolls—store bought and warm, buttery grits. And just as El had promised, it was delicious.

They sat across the table from each other making small talk, trying to pretend that nothing had changed since the night before, when in fact everything had changed and they both knew it.

"El?"

He glanced up at her, his mouth around a slice of bacon.

"I do love you."

He quickly chewed and swallowed. "I love you, too, baby." Using his fork, he cut into his scrambled eggs.

"I—I thought I could stop loving you. I was so angry with you. But I couldn't."

He put down his fork. "I know. What's brought all this up?"

She shook her head. "Nothing, I just want you to know, that I finally get it," she said and smiled softly. "No matter what happens, I will always love you. You're the one for me, even if you have to make some uncomfortable decisions."

He tilted his head and watched her for several moments, but before he could say anything the phone rang. He rose and went into the other room to answer it. It was Steve and he found himself in deep discussion with his attorney.

Steve had started out working for the firm that handled all of Carl's business; it was how the two had met. But after he went out on his own, Eliot had stayed with him. He'd needed a lawyer who would represent his interests and not necessarily his uncle's.

Because of that relationship, Steve still had many friends at the old firm and would often hear of things before they happened. Unfortunately, he was a couple of hours too late with his latest news.

Eliot quickly brought him up-to-date on his uncle's ultimatum and gave him his task before hanging up the phone. He started to turn back to the kitchen, then noticed a piece of paper sticking out of the drawer. He opened it and found the papers looking slightly more worn.

Slowly, he walked back into the kitchen and was only mildly surprised to find it empty. Suddenly, her strange, coded message made sense. *No matter what happens, I will always love you. You're the one for me, even if you have to make some uncomfortable decisions.*

Crazy woman, he thought. Did she seriously think he could chose his uncle's money over her ? Apparently, she did. With the shake of his head, he turned and headed back into his bedroom to dress. She had a little head start, not that it mattered. He knew exactly where to find her.

Later that afternoon, Carl sat in his attorney's office, never knowing an intern was listening in the hallway.

"Carl, are you sure about this? Don't you want to wait and see what he decides to do?"

"No," Carl sighed. Standing, he walked to the office window looking out over the city. "No, I'm done." A small smile came to his lips. "The rascal outsmarted me," he said.

"Then what was the purpose of the agreements you had me draw up?"

"Torture. Payback." Carl glanced at him. "Just my way of letting him know I could still stick it to him. But we both know I've planned for the boy to take over the company from the day he was born." He nodded, thinking to himself. "He turned out better than I thought he would, actually. A lot like me, despite his parents." He turned from the window. "Go ahead and draw up the will. I want to sign it as soon as possible. What do you think of Hawaii?"

"Hawaii?"

"As a retirement destination?"

"Retirement?!"

"I want to go somewhere warm."

"Carl, think about this. That company has been your life. Do you really just want to sign it over to someone who openly despises you and walk away?"

"That's the key right there. He despises *me,* not Fulton. Did you know what reasons he gave the clients to steal them away? He criticized my management and effectively challenged my leadership, but never once did he criticize the product of the company. He turned the customers off of me, not the company. He tells himself that me and the company are one and the same. But in his heart he separates us. Know why?"

"Why?"

"Because he loves the company, but if he didn't separate them in his heart that would mean loving me, too."

"Well, as long as you're sure about this."

"What do you think of the Caribbean?"

"Huh?"

"Retirement—"

"Destination. Right. I forgot."

Carl smiled at the man who'd taken care of his business matters for the past thirty years. "Look, I know there is a chance he will never talk to me again. There is even a chance he won't want to take over the company. But either way, I want him to have it to do with it what he will. Either way, I would prefer it in his hands, in the hands of a Fulton, even if his last name is Wright."

"Okay, I'll get the papers drawn up."

"I'm going to be in Miami for a few days. I'll sign them when I get back."

"Miami?"

"Yes, researching retire—"

"Never mind! I'll have the papers ready when you get back."

As he walked out of the office, Carl felt a certain lightness in his step. He'd already stopped the lawsuit. After all, if the girl was going to be his niece-in-law, he couldn't go around suing her. And he was pretty sure she was the one he saw peeking out from Eliot's bedroom that morning.

Some people might think he was wrong to present Eliot with the ultimatum, but like Carl told his lawyer, he was only trying to show the boy that he was not quite the toothless old dinosaur Eliot seemed to think he was.

He was leaving because he wanted to leave on his terms, under his conditions, even if those conditions had been precipitated by events put in motion by Eliot.

Carl had taught the boy everything he knew, and his current predicament only served to prove Eliot had been an excellent study. So now it was time to step aside and let the next generation take over. And he'd obviously chosen a woman who could stand by his side and help him run the business, seeing how she'd given them both a good run for their money in the beginning. Carl felt certain Fulton Foods was in good hands.

As he climbed into his car, Carl was considering a certain accountant named Marilyn. He wondered where was she now. She was a lovely older woman who'd audited them two years ago. As a result of late nights in the office, she and Carl had dinner brought in a few nights, and he found he enjoyed her company. But at the time, Carl had told himself he was too old to be considering anything more than a few late dinners.

But watching Eliot fall in love had done something to him. Had affected him in a way he never would have imagined. It started him thinking about the perfect retirement spot and wanting to visit some possible places. It had him understanding that with or without him, Fulton Foods would survive. And it had him thinking about that auditor and considering giving her a call.

Chapter 30

Sophie stopped by her home just long enough to change into a fresh set of clothes, then made one more stop before heading into the bakery.

As she walked into the kitchen, Wayne was loading an oven, and Mae was showing Lonnie how to cut out cookies. The girl was learning quickly, and Sophie realized all she'd ever needed was someone to show her how. No one had ever bothered because they'd all assumed she simply could not do it.

Everyone looked up as she walked in, then noticed the young man with her.

"Dante!" Lonnie dropped her cookie cutter and rushed across the room, throwing herself into his arms. Dante braced his thin frame for the impact and caught her up.

Lonnie spun to Mae and Wayne. "Look, it's Dante!"

But Mae and Wayne were both watching Sophie. She knew she should've offered some explanation for her mysterious disappearance the day before. But, the words were stuck in her throat, and she found herself unable to say anything for fear of bursting into tears. Instead, she turned and went into the office and no one followed her.

Determined not to think about El, Sophie threw herself into her work. By noon, she'd updated their supply list, cleaned out the walk-in refrigerator, found a repairman for the old oven and finished payroll for the week.

Sitting alone in the office, she was tempted to go into the front of the store and help Mae. But, she was afraid her grandmother would bombard her with questions. She wasn't ready to answer any just yet. So, when Dante dropped a bag of flour as he was loading it into the mixer, she offered to sweep it up. Something to do. Anything to keep from thinking about El. But it didn't work.

At various times throughout the morning, she imagined him entering Fulton Foods headquarters, dressed in one of his expensive suits, and walking straight into the executive suite. She had no idea what it looked like, but she could imagine…everything, right down to the beautiful smile on his face as he accepted his uncle's offer.

Mae was in the front of the store, handling the walk-ins. The rest of the group were putting together a medium-sized order for a new customer. Sophie wandered aimlessly around the kitchen, but no one said anything to her. In fact, they seemed to be avoiding talking to her as much as she was avoiding talking to them. When she passed Mae's cooking stove, she smiled to herself, realizing her grandmother was cooking a big pot of chicken and dumplings for lunch. Her grandma's chicken and dumplings had always been her favorite.

She watched Dante and Lonnie laughing in their connected way, and it soon became apparent that they'd been spending time together, even since Dante had been let go from the store. She didn't see how, considering Lonnie rarely ever went anywhere alone, but somehow they had. Some part of her wished her relationship with El were that simple.

It was around one when the front-door chime rang announcing a customer, and she heard Mae's laughter. Out of curiosity, Sophie wandered to the front of the store and stood frozen, as El and Mae talked and laughed liked old friends.

He wasn't wearing one of his expensive suits, and he certainly did not look like he'd just come from Fulton corporate headquarters.

Wearing jeans, sandals and a pullover shirt, he leaned against the counter and flirted shamelessly with her grandmother. Every so often he used the sunglasses in his hand to punctuate one of his points. And Mae was cooing like a schoolgirl and loving every minute of it.

He glanced at her with a smile. "Hey, baby."

"Hello." Sophie frowned, a little unsure how to greet him.

"I need to go check lunch," Mae said, coming from behind the counter. "You staying for lunch, El?"

"What are we having?" He winked at her.

"Like it matters with the way you eat," Mae said and laughed. "But, just so you know, chicken and dumplings."

"Oh, definitely!"

"Thought so." Mae chuckled and shook her head, heading into the kitchen.

"What are you doing here?" Sophie asked, coming farther into the store.

He continued to lean on the counter, but turned to face her. "I could ask you the same question. Why'd you take off so fast this morning?"

She shrugged. "Had a lot to do."

"Really?" He frowned thoughtfully. "And here I thought it had something to do with those documents my uncle left me. You know…the ones in my desk drawer."

Sophie knew he realized she'd read them, but she wasn't about to condemn herself with a confession. So, she stayed silent.

"Oh, you don't know what I'm talking about, huh?" He glanced out the front window. "Can we go somewhere and talk?"

She looked out the window. "What's wrong with right here?"

"Too many ears." He glanced over her shoulder.

Sophie turned, surprised to see Wayne leaning against the kitchen entrance. His eyes shooting daggers at El. "Fine. Wayne, can you tell Grandma I'll be back in a short while?"

Wayne nodded slowly before turning to walk back into the

kitchen. El held the door open for her, and as she stepped outside Sophie realized the weather had taken a slight turn since she'd entered that morning. The sun had disappeared behind dark clouds, as if reflecting her mood.

"Going to be an early fall," El said, as if reading her mind.

She glanced up at the gray sky, and nodded in agreement. "Where to?"

He smiled. "The Icy Palace down the street is open."

Sophie nodded again, trying desperately not to be charmed by his beautiful smile. It had been her downfall from the moment she met him.

They'd walked a few feet in silence then he finally said, "Sophie, I know you read the papers, and I think I know why you left. But I'd rather hear it from you."

"Hear what?"

He stopped and turned to her. "Fine, you want to play it like that. Then I'll say it. No, I had no intention of accepting my uncle's offer to take over the company—although it's a moot point now. I would've never signed those papers."

"Why not?"

He frowned at her. "Do you really think so little of me? That I would throw away what we have for money?"

She placed a hand on her hip and leaned toward him. "You came into my bakery and pretended to be my friend and lover for almost four months—for money! It's not such a great leap."

"Okay, that's it! You have to decide right here and right now. You can forgive me for that stupid, stupid mistake…and we go on and build a life together, or… we let this go right now. I can't spend my entire life telling you I'm sorry. You know I am." He turned to walk away, but came right back to within an inch of her face. "And I *won't* allow you to hang this over me for the rest of my life!"

She glared at him. "You have no idea how it feels to bare your soul to someone and know all the time that he's laughing at you. It's hard for me to let that go, El."

He took both her hands in his. "I never laughed at you. Never! How can you think that?"

"Then why didn't you tell me the truth?"

"Because I'm an idiot. I thought I could hide it forever and you would never have to know. But never doubt that the guilt was eating me up inside."

"Then why didn't you tell me?"

Seeing the water in her eyes, El pulled her into his arms. "Shh, don't cry," he said and he kissed the top of her head. "I'm so sorry I hurt you. If I could undo it I would."

Sophie wrapped her arms around his midsection, holding him tight. "I just don't want to be blindsided again, El."

"You won't be. But I meant what I said. You've got to find some way to forgive me and to trust me, or this will never work."

"I trust you…that's the problem. I *do* trust you, but some part of me thinks I shouldn't."

He put his arm around her shoulder, and they started walking again. "When I first arrived at my uncle's house, I was totally unprepared for what life with him would be like. I had been raised with loving, caring parents, who went out of their way to avoid hurting me. And suddenly, here I was with this man who thought hurting me was his job. He said it would make me tough." His full lips pulled in a flat line. "I learned quickly, and maybe got a little too good at taking the blows. After a while, his way of looking at the world started to make sense to me. I started buying what he was selling." He looked down at the ground, trying to form his thoughts. "When I came here—" he gestured around them "—to Selmer, to the bakery, and met you and your grandmother, it reminded me of the home I grew up in. The people I knew then. My father's family, our neighbors and friends. And I realized how much I'd missed that life. I was afraid to lose it."

"So your answer was to stick your head in the sand, and wait for your crazy uncle to tell me?"

"No, I had no idea he planned to come here. Although, looking back, I should have. It's just like him. But I was hoping to find a way to stop him, neutralize him before he could do any harm." He stopped and turned her toward him again. "I blinked, and he caught me unaware."

"So, what are you saying, El? You've been playing these mind games with your uncle for so long I'm afraid that you can't stop. Can you just walk away from all that?"

"Yes."

"Yes? Just like that?"

"Just like that. I'll prove it. He has signed the company over to me."

She frowned. "I thought you said you didn't—"

"I didn't. He changed his will and has officially announced his retirement. But I have no intention of taking over the company."

"Then what will happen to it?"

"I'm going to option stock to the employees and set up a board of directors."

"El? This is your family's business."

"Not anymore." He turned her toward the bakery a block behind them. *"That's our family business."*

Without turning to look at him, she asked, "But can that be enough for you?"

"As long as you're there. You're not only enough for me, you're more than I dreamed I'd find." He turned her back to face him. "I love you, Sophie. Is that enough for you?"

She smiled. "How can it not be? You're my Mr. Wright."

A love that's out of this world…

Cosmic Rendezvous

Favorite author
Robyn Amos

For aerospace engineer Shelly London, a top-secret
space project could be her big break—until she butts
heads with sexy hotshot astronaut Lincoln Ripley, who
launches her hormones right into orbit. Lincoln's got
a double mission: catch a saboteur…then take off with
Shelly for a rendezvous with love.

"Lilah's List is…a fun story that
holds one's interest from page one."
—*Romantic Times BOOKreviews*

*Coming the first week of April 2009
wherever books are sold.*

KIMANI™
ROMANCE

The "Triple Threat" Donovan brothers are back…
and last-man-standing Trent is about to roll the
dice on falling in love.

Defying
DESIRE

Book #3 in *The Donovan Brothers*

A.C. Arthur

When it comes to men, model Tia St. Claire wants no
strings, just flings. But navy SEAL Trent Donovan stirs
defiant longings she can't deny. Happily unattached,
Trent has dedicated his career to duty and danger, until
desire—and Tia—changes everything.

"If hero Adam Donovan was for sale, every woman in
the world would be lined up to buy him!"
—*Romantic Times BOOKreviews* on
A CINDERELLA AFFAIR

Coming the first week of April 2009
wherever books are sold.

KIMANI™
ROMANCE

www.kimanipress.com
www.myspace.com/kimanipress   KPACA1090409

REQUEST YOUR FREE BOOKS!

2 FREE NOVELS
PLUS 2 *FREE GIFTS!*

KIMANI™
ROMANCE

Love's ultimate destination!

KROM08R

A dazzling story of a woman forced to decide where her heart really lies…

AWARD-WINNING AUTHOR

ADRIANNE BYRD

Love
takes time

All her life, Alyssa Jansen has loved handsome, wealthy Quentin Dwayne Hinton—a man who barely knows she exists. Now after years away in France, Alyssa's back, and Q is seeing her in a whole new light. But so is his brother Sterling, a handsome and passionate man who is willing to give Alyssa what she wants. Suddenly Alyssa must choose between a fairy tale come true and a new, unexpected love….

Coming the first week of April 2009 wherever books are sold.

ARABESQUE®

www.kimanipress.com
www.myspace.com/kimanipress

KPAB1170409